Aikur's War

By

Sam Ferguson

AIKUR'S WAR

Copyright © 2018 by Sam Ferguson
Artwork Copyright © 2018 Dragon Scale Publishing

ISBN 13: 978-1943183449
ISBN 10: 1943183449

Published by Dragon Scale Publishing
Front Cover Art by Luciano Fleitas

For Lexie, Maurice, Bob, and Levi.

Other Books by Sam Ferguson:

The Dragon's Champion Series
The Sorceress of Aspenwood Series
Son of the Dragon
The Dragons of Kendualdern Series
The Fur Trader 1 & 2
The Haymaker Adventures
Hapless Heroes Series
Flight of the Krilo
The Ghosts of Kobhir
Gatekeepers
The Lost City of Alfarin
Wren and the Ravens
The Moon Dragon
The Beast of Blue Mountain

Other Books by Dragon Scale Publishing:

The Protector of Esparia by Lisa M. Wilson
Wisp the Wayfinder and Other Tales by J.M. Hauser
Kingdom of Denall Series by Eric Buffington:
Blood Bound by B. Griffin
Blood Penance by B. Griffin
Favored by B. Griffin
The Bohemian Magician by A.L. Sirois
Tharzule's Tome of Wishes by Malinda Smiley
Codex of Light by E.P. Stein
Codex of Darkness by E.P. Stein
The Dream Chest by E.P. Stein

For more, check out Dragon Scale Publishing's website:
www.DragonScaleBooks.com

Table of Contents

Prologue

Thunder rolled across the purple and black clouds. An acrid, stale odor permeated the darkened air below as Lysander's chest heaved for breath. Fireballs tore through the atmosphere, roaring as they passed overhead and left columns of gray and black smoke in their wake.

Icadion, the All-Father, was bleeding from his left arm, and his strength was draining. He cast his eyes about the battlefield and then turned to his son. "The demons are too strong," he said. "We must pull back."

"Father, no!" Lysander cried. "If we leave, then we will be abandoning the world to the Four Horsemen."

"It is too late," Icadion shouted. "The Sacred Dark has been unleashed upon the land by your brother, and there is nothing we can do now to stop it from spreading."

Off in the distance there was laughter as a massive blue demon with wings of fire swept his blade through an army of men. Scores fell with one swing, their screams filling the air for only a moment before the demon's crimson heart of crystal glowed bright and pulled their souls in.

"Soulfin grows stronger with every life he takes," Icadion said. "Only the Four Horsemen can stop him!"

"NO!" Lysander shouted. "I will not leave these people. I have grown among them, and come to love them."

"We can create a new world!" Icadion shouted. "Do not let your emotions rule you. You are a god, act like one!"

Lysander stood and drew his powerful sword, Myrskyn. "For the first time in my life, I *am* acting like one," he said. "I will not leave!"

A four-legged beast lunged at Icadion from the side, but the All-Father turned and drove his spear into the demon's head, killing it instantly and spraying the ground with a shower of black blood as the spear exploded through the creature's head. The creator of Terramyr then flung the corpse back toward a group of twelve such demons before calling down seven bolts of lightning that blasted through the others.

"My energy is spent," Icadion said. "Even a god must rest. If you stay here, I will be forced to leave you behind. Hildervahl will close Bifrost as soon as I have crossed back to Volganor."

"Then, until we meet again, Father," Lysander said. He turned back to the battlefield and rushed down the hill, his tired legs pounding the hard-packed dirt and his lungs burning for reprieve. All around him, men, elves, dwarves, and other creatures threw themselves endlessly at the creatures spewing forth from the bowels of hell. A nine-foot tall ogre charged him, wielding a club, but Lysander easily dodged the blow and countered with a single thrust of his sword to the ogre's neck. Dark blood ran down the enchanted blade for only a second before Lysander used the magic to call down a massive storm of lightning that blasted the ogre's body away from him.

"We can't let that thing through!" someone shouted from Lysander's right. He turned and saw Jaeger, a powerful gnome warrior who had come with him to the great battle against Atek and his minions. "That demon will crush everything if he crosses the mountains," Jaeger shouted.

A goblin rushed in, screaming and wailing as it readied its axe, but Jaeger turned and drove his spear into the green-skinned warrior's face and forced the goblin to the ground.

A tall orc stepped in to attack Jaeger while the gnome yanked his spear free, but there was a wet, *thabunk!*

The orc went rigid and then fell to the side, revealing Drenylin, a stout dwarf with a reputation nearly as fierce as that of the gods themselves.

"I'm with you if you want to make a run for the thing," Drenylin called out.

Lysander nodded. "We may not win, but we can at least give the others time to pull back. They can form a better defensive line within the Nahktun Mountains. In the open field, the demon is unstoppable, but in the narrow crags the others might be able to bring it down."

"Well, if the three of you are about to commit suicide, then I suppose I had better join you," a familiar voice rang out over the din of battle.

Lysander turned to see a tall elf and smiled. "Lysander and the warriors three, it has a good ring to it," he said with a nod.

"I prefer Yaen and his lackeys, but I suppose you can name the group just this once," the elf replied.

Lysander turned and watched as the demon swept through a contingent of cavalry numbering at least fifty strong. "We have to sound the retreat. The more he kills, the stronger he becomes."

Wings beat the air overhead and then the ground shook as Nagé dropped to the dirt before Lysander and bowed to him. "My prince, it is not my place to command you, but I must remind you that Soulfin can kill you."

Lysander smirked. "The demon can do more than that," Lysander said. "He can destroy the entire world."

"You brother Atek is defeated. If you return with us, we can protect Volganor from Soulfin. There is no need to risk your life, my prince."

Lysander summoned lightning and fire to sweep aside a small number of orcs and goblins that were marching up the hill toward him and the others. "Soulfin doesn't only destroy the bodies of those he kills, he is eating their souls. I cannot run away from such an abomination."

Nagé nodded. "Neither can I," she said.

"Nagé, if you stay here, Bifrost will close without you."

"I have three hundred Valkyries at my command." She rose and stretched her wings proudly while stamping the butt of her silver spear on the ground. "I was given the task of collecting the honorable dead from Terramyr. That is not a duty I can reject now. If you stay, then I stay as well."

A flash of silver split the air between them, accompanied by a crash of thunder. A tall man in a green cloak stepped out from the light, holding a pair of spears. As Lysander brought his arm away from his eyes he motioned for the others to stay their weapons. Each of the warriors present lowered their arms a bit, but no one put them away.

"I thought you couldn't interfere," Lysander said.

"I have two spears," Reshem said, avoiding the other question. "They are made with the horn of a special ram. The golden horns come from a realm far from here, and they are able to destroy beings made from Sacred Dark."

Nagé's mouth fell open and she glanced to Lysander.

"Are you saying this can slay the demon?" Lysander asked, ignoring Nagé's uncomfortable stare.

"I believe so," Reshem said.

"He doesn't sound that confident," Drenylin put in. The dwarf hocked a loogie and then spat onto the ground.

"I have enough confidence that I am willing to go into battle with you," Reshem said. He held out one of the spears for Lysander. "If I am right, then this horn can not only slay Soulfin, but it will destroy his very soul. More than that, this weapon has the power to fight with ghosts."

"Ghosts, why would we want that ability?" Jaeger shouted. "The tall one is mad." Jaeger made a circling gesture with his finger beside his head and crossed his eyes.

"The orcs that die, are their spirits not gathered into an army in Hammenfein?" Reshem asked.

Lysander nodded, knowing already where this logic was going. "So if Hatmul decides to unleash the ghost armies, we will have a way to defend ourselves."

"If Hatmul unleashes thousands of ghosts, two spears isn't going to do much of anything," Drenylin said.

"We don't have much time," Reshem said.

Lysander looked to the others and then back to Reshem. "What about the other Watchers?"

Reshem smirked and offered a shrug as his only answer. "You should take the spear."

Lysander tossed his sword to Jaeger. "See that you take care of this."

The gnome caught the blade and gave it a practice swing. "It will be an honor to fight alongside you."

Lysander shook his head. "Change of plans. I have Nagé and Reshem at my side. You three help the armies retreat. See that you lead them to safety across the mountains. The Valkyries will assist you."

Drenylin and Jaeger started to protest, but Yaen stepped in. "This is the wisest action. We can save many if we act quickly."

"I shall have the Valkyries cut a swath through Atek's armies, and then the others will be able to make a run for the mountains," Nagé said. The tall goddess closed her eyes and bowed her head. A moment later Valkyries filled the sky and flew in unison.

Lysander offered a final nod to his friends, and then he, Nagé, and Reshem held hands.

"This might sting a bit," Reshem mentioned. A flash of silver light blinded Lysander as the ground fell away below him. The wind ripped at his hair and clothes and then everything stopped, as if the world came to a complete stand still. Lysander looked down as another flash of silver light deposited him in the air a few feet above Soulfin's head. Nagé flew out to the side, her wings gliding effortlessly as she pulled a bow and began firing at the blue-skinned beast below.

Lysander, second son of Icadion, fell through the air and pointed his spear downward, hoping to land a solid blow and drive his weapon through the demon's skull. A second flash of silver exploded off to the side, and Lysander could just make out Reshem as the tall man lunged in for Soulfin's ankle.

Time moved slowly at first. A fall that should have spanned only a second or two seemed to stretch out for much longer as the demon turned his head upward. Nagé's arrows flew sluggishly through the air, spinning and turning at a fraction of the rate they should have.

Inexplicably, time lurched forward. The arrows zipped downward and Lysander crashed into the demon's head, only the spear did not penetrate the beast's skull. Instead, the tip of the ram's golden horn tore through the thin layer of flesh and then bounced off the solid skull beneath. The demon took a swipe at Lysander, forcing the mortalized god to leap out of the way. It was a seventy foot drop to the ground, but Nagé was there in an instant, catching Lysander and then darting back and away from Soulfin as the creature swatted at her with one of his fiery wings. The wing itself missed, but it created a wake of searing hot air that forced Nagé to fly even farther away.

"Reshem is down there, we have to get in for another attack," Lysander cried out.

He watched as Reshem stabbed Soulfin's ankle twice, spraying blood that looked more like glowing, red-hot magma out onto the ground.

The demon raised his foot and moved to stomp Reshem into oblivion, but the Watcher vanished, teleporting before the foot could drop. A flash of silver opened up in

Nagé's path and the goddess let out a startled scream before trying to turn to the side. Reshem reached out and grabbed Lysander's forearm and in another flash of light the two were transported away, leaving Nagé flying alone in the air.

Reshem deposited Lysander on Soulfin's left side, forty yards away from the demon, and then he smiled at the god. "I will draw his eyes. Wait for your moment, and then strike."

Soulfin turned and focused on Nagé. An orb of black formed in the beast's open mouth, and Lysander knew what was happening next. The demon would unleash a powerful spell that would suck the living soul out of any creature it touched. It had already consumed several lower level gods and countless others with this same power.

Lysander stood to call for Nagé, but Reshem teleported to her and snatched her away in an instant, pulling her out of harm's way just as the black orb shot out from Soulfin's mouth, crackling with electrical energy as it grew and tore through the air.

A flash of silver appeared high in the sky over the demon, and then there was a second just atop the demon's shoulder. Lysander had to keep from shouting out as Reshem drove his spear into the base of the demon's neck. Soulfin spun around, but Reshem had already teleported down to the ground. A moment later Soulfin roared angrily as Reshem tore a gash in the demon's foot. Nagé fired several enchanted arrows from above, blasting Soulfin with missiles that called down lightning from the heavens and drilled into his flesh while the Watcher continued to teleport around the beast and harass it with quick stabs and stinging slices.

Soulfin snarled and desperately lashed out through the air in an attempt to catch Reshem, but the Watcher somehow always appeared in a safe place just long enough to jab Soulfin and then take off again.

The only problem was that no matter how many times the demon was struck, it didn't seem to tire. The wounds Nagé inflicted upon the beast healed up only seconds after they had been made, and even though it appeared that Soulfin could not heal the areas Reshem had struck, the injuries did not seem to do much more than anger the beast.

A few moments later, a dozen Valkyries flew in from the south. Their spears and bows gleamed brightly under the light of Nagé's magical attacks. Reshem focused his teleportations away from Soulfin to keep the beast focused on him, but it was no use. Soulfin must have heard the winged warriors coming. He flexed his mighty, fiery wings and sent a wall of flame up that consumed the first six Valkyries. The others turned away, but even as Reshem kept poking and stabbing the beast, Soulfin spun around and caught two more Valkyries with his sword, and devoured the last four with his orb spell, sucking their souls away for all eternity.

Nagé wept and charged in from above, firing her bow so rapidly that Soulfin flinched away from the unrelenting lightning.

Reshem continued his assault, focusing on the demon's shoulders.

Lysander stood up, ready to strike. With Nagé coming in from high above and blasting the demon in the face, Soulfin was already arching upward, exposing much of his torso. Reshem's attack forced the beast to raise its arms and wings up to counter, meaning Lysander would have a clear shot, but the window of opportunity would be brief.

Had Lysander not been born into a mortal life upon Terramyr, he would have retained all of his former glory, and he could have traveled the distance in the blink of an eye, but not now. Though he had magical weapons and extraordinary strength and agility, he had none of the powers he had once wielded as a god. He didn't even have any magical ability, for those things had been stripped from him for his mortal probation.

"Father, just this once, grant me a portion of your strength!" Lysander whispered, hoping that his small prayer would be answered, and then he charged across the battlefield. His feet felt light upon the darkened ground, but he knew in his heart that he could never reach Soulfin in time. Nagé was closing in much faster, and would be forced to turn away or suffer ultimate destruction, and Reshem was running out of safe places to appear along Soulfin's mighty shoulders. Another three seconds, and the demon would surely kill one of the two, if not both.

"PLEASE!" Lysander grunted through his tightly clench teeth.

An explosion of light sent myriad colors out over the darkened field and scattered the purple and black clouds from the sky just long enough for a thick, golden bolt of lightning to streak across and down to Lysander.

"Aim true, my son," Icadion's low voice instructed as the lightning snaked beneath Lysander and lifted him upward, rocketing toward Soulfin's chest.

The demon lost interest in Nagé and Reshem. It turned toward Lysander, but Lysander held true to his objective, aiming his spear for the demon's heart. Riding the writhing, charged force beneath him, he managed to pierce the demon's chest. Thunder rumbled over the valley and tremors rocked the ground below as Lysander's great spear plunged deep into Soulfin's heart. There, instead of a heart of flesh, was a solid, pulsing crystal behind the demon's protective ribcage. The spear exploded upon impact, showering Lysander in shards of crystal as Icadion's lightning bored deeper into the hole Lysander had made.

Soulfin gnashed his teeth and fell to the ground. His fiery wings broke apart as if made of nothing more than ash fighting a hurricane wind and scattering out over the land behind him, poisoning the ground it touched. The demon's blue skin melted away to reveal thick cords of muscle that hissed and smoked once exposed to the elements. Reshem teleported down and drove his spear into the same hole as well. It caught the last bit of crystalline heart remaining inside and created a terrible explosion.

Lysander was thrown several yards away, and Reshem only barely managed to teleport himself out of harm's way before green flames erupted and consumed the rest of Soulfin's flesh.

Nagé landed beside Lysander and stretched out her hand over his forehead. Lysander shook and trembled, but as the goddess' powers flowed through him his body calmed and grew still.

"Is it over?" Lysander asked.

Reshem appeared at his side in a flash of silver and knelt down. "You have been struck by a few of the shards," he said.

"I'm all right," Lysander replied as he looked to his torn shoulder.

"No, you won't be," Reshem said. "If you're lucky, you will only go mad, but you could die from this."

"I can heal you," Nagé said as she continued to pour her powers into Lysander.

Lysander pushed himself up and looked out over the small crater in the ground. "There is something there," he said. The others looked to where he was pointing. A glowing crystal stood on its point, spinning in the center of the crater.

"That is the Astral Crystal," Reshem said.

"From the creation?" Lysander asked. The ex-god rose to his feet and looked around. Most of the orcs and other cursed races were scattering, running away at the sight of Soulfin's defeat, but the lesser demons were only partially frightened. They were like a pack of dogs that had been

10

chased off by a bear, scared and running away, but they would regroup quickly once they realized they had the advantage in numbers.

"It has to be protected," Reshem said. The Watcher turned to Lysander. "You must take it, and hide it."

"What? Why me? You said my wounds would…" Lysander winced and grabbed his arm as a burning pain ripped through his shoulder. The sensation left as quickly as it had begun.

"Your heroes have done well," Reshem said. "They have made it possible for the others to retreat. Take them with you, go somewhere to hide the crystal, and then charge them with its safe keeping. If you live through the madness that Soulfin's poison will inflict upon you, then you can return for the crystal."

"I can take it," Nagé said with a decisive nod. "It will be safe with me."

"No," Reshem said quickly. "When I leave this place, I will have to report to the Cosmic Council. If they were to discover that such an artifact had already given rise to a creature like Soulfin, they would investigate further. If that investigation revealed that you held the crystal while other gods fled the world, then it would mean the end of Terramyr."

"Doesn't the Cosmic Council already know about Soulfin?" Nagé asked.

Reshem took in a deep breath and shook his head. "No. I have already lost a world. I will not lose another."

"You haven't told the Council about any of the missing crystals have you?"

Reshem shook his head. "If they knew the Crystals of Power were unaccounted for…"

Nagé nodded. "I still don't understand why *I* can't have it," she said.

"Because," Lysander said. "You are not of appropriate station to safeguard the crystal. Khullan was."

"*You* aren't of an appropriate level either, my prince. Forgive me, but you are no more than a fallen god now."

"Better Icadion's son than the collector of the dead," Reshem said. "Now come, we have no more time."

Lysander nodded. "I will help them hide the crystal."

Reshem grabbed Lysander's arms and the two of them vanished, only to appear an instant later next to the spinning crystal. Lysander reached down and took the cold crystal in hand.

"To think that Soulfin was made by joining the Sacred Dark to this crystal…" Lysander whispered.

"Come, I will carry you to a place I know near Tanglewood Forest. You will be safe there while I make arrangements for you." Reshem teleported Lysander hundreds of miles in less than a second, and set the injured ex-god down upon a large, gray stone. "I will be back with the others." Reshem vanished. A few moments later he reappeared with Drenylin.

"That wasn't so bad," Drenylin said as he straightened his belt. The dwarf walked two steps, and then turned to retch on the ground.

"The feeling will pass quickly," Reshem said before vanishing again.

Next he returned with Yaen, the elf.

Yaen went straight to Lysander. "I have some herbs," Yaen said. "I will help you, master."

"There is nothing for it," Reshem said as Yaen quickly made a poultice and applied it to Lysander's arm and shoulder. The Watcher then teleported away once more and returned with Jaeger.

Once all three comrades had been reunited with Lysander, Reshem spoke up. "Listen, the ram from which I took the horns can help you still. I will find it and take it to a village northeast of here, deep inside Tanglewood Forest."

"Ram horns?" Jaeger asked. "You mean the same ram horns you used to make the spears before?"

Lysander patted the air and nodded. "I can explain later." He turned back to Reshem. "How will the ram help us?"

"The magic in his horns dispel magic born of the Sacred Dark. So long as the animal's horns are kept nearby, the crystal can be effectively hidden from the demons and any of Atek's minions' sight. I will go and procure the ram, and then I will take it to the village northeast of here. You will know it when you see it, for it is an albino, and it is much larger than any other ram in these parts of Terramyr. Go there as soon as you are able to travel, but you must take care. The ram will shed its horns every hundred years and grow a new set. Each time this happens, you will replace the old pair of horns with the new, this will ensure that the magic is always as potent as possible, for the demons will never cease their search for the crystal. As long as you keep the animal close to the village and keep it protected, you should always be able to conceal the crystal's existence."

"Rams don't shed their horns," Jaeger said dismissively.

"This ram does not come from Terramyr, and it does shed its horns. Remember, gather the new horns every hundred years."

"I will remember," Lysander said."

Reshem nodded and smiled. "I hope the sickness will pass from you quickly, but caution you that it may be centuries before you regain all of your strength, Lysander."

"We'll keep him safe," Yaen responded dutifully.

"We won't leave his side, not even for a day," Drenylin added.

"Very well," Reshem said. "I must leave you all now. Good luck, and may the fates be kind. I will return as soon as I can."

Lysander nodded and waved, but Reshem was already gone. The ex-god leaned to the side and brought out the crystal. "You did well leading the others out of the valley, but now we have a new assignment." He winced and jerked to the side as pain shot down along his spine.

"Master, are you all right?" Yaen asked.

Lysander shook his head and held the crystal out for Yaen.

Drenylin stepped up and snatched it away. "I know every kind of gem, jewel, and crystal on Terramyr, but I have never seen anything like this before in my life."

"It's one of the Crystals of Power," Lysander said. "It was used to make Soulfin."

"How did you find it?" Jaeger asked, stepping forward and leaning in to inspect the jewel.

"It was buried in the center of Soulfin's heart, which was itself a crystal that formed around this one," Lysander answered. "We have to—"

Giiiiiiiyaaaaaah!

The screech rang out over the plains as loudly as though it had been only a few feet away.

Lysander stood on his feet. "Jaeger, give me Myrskyn."

"But, you can barely stand," Jaeger replied. "Let me handle the demon."

"There's more than one of them," Drenylin shouted as he whipped out his axe and pointed off to the side.

Lysander turned and felt his heart drop as columns of black fire rose from the ground all around them. Some of the monsters had long, scythe-like arms of sharp bone, others were massive with hundreds of legs and sharp pincers and fangs, and others were winged imps.

14

"Protect the crystal at all costs," Lysander said. "If it falls into the wrong hands, the Cosmic Council could learn of it and come to handle the situation themselves."

"You mean send the Four Horsemen," Yaen put in.

A wyvern appeared in a puff of smoke nearby and swooped in toward Lysander. The ex-god spun around with Myrskyn and cut the demon in two, showering the ground in hissing, black blood.

Drenylin charged a four-legged thing that looked like a bear, but had a scorpion's tail. The stinger came down, but the stout dwarf chopped the tail off by a third and then spun around to sink his axe into the beast's left shoulder. Yaen came in hard and fast, casting a fireball that disoriented the beast and then driving a spear into its eye. Jaeger let out a cry to Mother Terramyr and went to work, nimbly dashing between the legs of larger beasts and stabbing them in the groin, stomach, or any other soft spot he could manage to reach.

Lysander cut down a large snake slithering toward him, and then he called forth Myrskyn's lightning to zap a trio of humanoid demons before they could unleash their fireball spells at him.

For a time, Lysander was certain they would be victorious, but as Drenylin engaged a tall, slender demon that walked upon hooved feet and wielded a fire-whip, the demon snatched the crystal from him and somehow accessed its power. A great earthquake ripped the ground apart. Fireballs fell from the sky, pummeling the ground and exploding in great gobs of deadly magma. Drenylin tried to retake the crystal, but a beast that looked like a panther leapt out from an opening chasm and took him to the ground. Drenylin shouted and grunted, but Lysander could see it wouldn't end well. He charged forward and drove Myrskyn through the panther's neck and then kicked the beast off of his friend.

15

Jaeger sprinted into the fray, ducking under a fireball just enough to avoid losing his head as the massive thing left a crater behind him and sprayed a nearby demon with magma. The gnome darted around demons and fireballs alike until he reached the fleeing demon with the crystal. He planted his spear up into the demon's lower back, going straight through the kidneys and out the abdominal wall. The demon spun around and struck Jaeger with the fiery whip, knocking the gnome across the ground, but this gave Yaen just enough time to cast a spell that froze the spear stuck inside the winged demon. The ice creaked and cracked as the demon snarled and tried to fight against the cold, but it was no use. The demon fell to its knees.

Drenylin rushed in and struck the frozen spear, shattering it into hundreds of razor-like shards that ripped through the demon's torso. As it tried to lash out at the dwarf, Drenylin came in hard and swift with his axe, killing the monster and regaining the crystal in the process.

Lysander poured his focus into Myrskyn, calling down lightning in the greatest storm the ex-god had ever summoned. Explosions rocked the area as the earthquake intensified. The very ground started to groan in protest as Terramyr was ripped apart and scarred. Lysander and his comrades fell into a widening chasm, tumbling and rolling down the sides until they landed hard on the rocky bottom. A river that had been nearby before the earthquake was now pouring over into the canyons, and soon Lysander and the others were swept away. Yaen's magic kept them all afloat until they came to a tall, thick column of stone that stood alone in the middle of the canyons, like a proud tower that refused to bend to the earthquake's power.

"Here," Yaen said as he summoned his magic to lift them all from the fierce, newborn river. "Jaeger, help me with this."

Lysander leaned against a boulder and watched as the gnome and elf used their magic to turn the pillar into an actual tower, creating an entrance on the south side.

"We can shelter in here," Yaen said.

"I can scout ahead, see if there is a way out of here," Jaeger announced before jumping down to a log that was floating upon the river. "I'll be back soon. Get Lysander into the tower and keep him safe."

Lysander wanted to speak. He tried to warn his friend that scouting alone would be dangerous, but his jaw wouldn't obey his mind. It shivered as though he was racked by chills, but in reality his forehead was dripping with sweat, and he could barely focus his eyes, for it felt as though his head would lift off from his neck and float away.

"Come, Master," Yaen said as he slipped under Lysander's uninjured arm and pulled the ex-god to a standing position. "We'll be safe inside the tower. We have cast many wards upon it. The demons will not find us inside."

"We can use the crystal," Drenylin said just as Yaen and Lysander reached the entrance to the tower. The dwarf walked out away from them and stood upon a large rock that was not yet covered by the rushing waters. "I can use it the same way that demon did, and I'll send the buggers all back to Hammenfein where they belong."

Lysander mouthed the word "No," but his voice was gone.

Whatever Drenylin tried, it didn't work. A deafening explosion threw out purple and silver flames and a shockwave that struck Lysander and threw the ex-god and Yaen into the tower with such force that they lost consciousness. The report echoed across the canyon several times, and then all went still.

"Master, can you hear me?" Jaeger called.

Lysander opened his eyes, but could only make out Jaeger's outline. "Drenylin…used…crystal…"

"I know. I found it. I have it here," Jaeger said, bringing the crystal up in front of Lysander's eyes.

"How long…"

"I heard the explosion several minutes ago. It took me some time to make my way back against the river's current."

"Drenylin?" Lysander asked in a whisper.

"Dead," Jaeger responded. "I found only the lower half of his right leg upon a rock. The rest of him was gone. The crystal was lying between two stones, trapped by the current."

"Yaen?" Lysander asked.

Jaeger nodded. "He is unconscious, but alive."

Lysander arched up suddenly, his back thrown into a spasm by a flash of pain ripping down his spine. "Gyah!" Lysander snarled as a second, more forceful wave of cramps hit him. "Did you find a way out?"

"I did."

"Then go," Lysander said. "The demons will come for me, and I will make my last stand here. You must take the crystal to safety."

"I can't leave both of you here," Jaeger protested.

Lysander grabbed Jaeger's hand and put it on Myrskyn's handle. "Take this, and it will serve you well."

"What about you?" Jaeger asked.

"Go…protect the crystal. When I am able, I will come for it."

"And what if you aren't able?" Jaeger asked.

"Then I will send another champion in my place, and he will carry my bow as a token of my authority."

Jaeger nodded. "Until we meet again, Lysander, Protector of Men."

Lysander smiled weakly and then coughed up a small amount of blood. "Go to the north, as Reshem told us. Find the village of which he spoke, and the magical albino ram will help you hide the crystal."

Chapter 1

The sound of laughter tickled Aikur's ears. The large man took a break from chopping wood, set his axe down next to the pile, and went to find his wife and son playing in the garden. He stopped and leaned against the corner of his home, admiring his wife. Karyna was as lovely as the day was long. Dark skin and darker eyes set beneath locks of jet black hair. Their son was the spitting image of her, which in Aikur's estimation was a good thing. The boy would have his father's build, but his mother's face. The retired warrior could only hope that Dezri would have his mother's intelligence and disposition as well.

"Butterfly!" Dezri shouted as he stood up on his chubby toddler legs and stomped his way across the grass, lost in his hopeless pursuit of the butterfly that managed to stay several feet away from him.

"Dezri, you'll catch the butterfly with cunning, not with speed," Karyna said.

Aikur watched as Karyna gently plucked a large, red flower and then held it up. The toddler turned and grinned as the butterfly flew up and over him, then down to the flower his mother held out.

"And that is how you captured my heart," Aikur said.

"I didn't use a flower with you," Karyna said with a wink as the butterfly vigorously flapped its wings and left the garden.

"No, but what is a flower to a butterfly if not food? You offered me croc steak with red asparagus and ash potatoes. I was trapped from the very first bite."

Dezri waddled over to his mother and took the flower from her hands, giggling and chattering on about the butterfly.

"Be careful of women-folk, Dezri, for they will use their wiles against you," Aikur said.

"And have you regretted it?" Karyna asked as she rose to her feet and brushed off her green skirt.

Aikur shook his head and took her in his arms. "Not for a moment." He leaned in and kissed her softly. Dezri came in hard, wedging his head between the pair as if he were a miniature bull. Aikur pulled back as his son territorially reached around Karyna's legs and held on tight.

"I thought you would be back with the council by now," Karyna said.

Aikur frowned and glanced over his shoulder to the road. It was expected for a Konnon to live for battle. They were a hard people, raised from the ashes of the harshest environments Terramyr had to offer. There was a part of him that longed to go. He took in a deep breath and let it out slowly. "My place is here now, with you."

Karyna reached out and caressed Aikur's cheek with her hand. "We left New Konnland to make a new life for ourselves, but you don't have to give up everything."

Aikur smiled. "No, I should stay with you and Dezri. They have enough men to guard the border from a few goblins."

"I saw the disappointment in their eyes when you turned them down," Karyna said.

"Let them be disappointed," Aikur replied. "My fighting days are done." He swept his hand out toward their house. "That is why we sailed away from New Konnland, and came here after all, to build a new life. Think of it, in only one more year, our Dezri would have been starting at his first war training school. By the age of six, he would have been ranked against the others. At the age of twelve, he

21

would have been assigned to his first patrol, scouring the wastelands for Kottri and minotaurs." Aikur frowned and shook his head. "But not here. Here we are free to live in peace."

Karyna nodded and then grabbed Aikur's chin. "I also saw the disappointment in *your* eyes, my love. I know you want a better life for us, and you are working so hard to make it a reality, but I am worried you may lose yourself by denying who you are."

"You would have me go and fight the goblins in the mountains?" Aikur asked skeptically.

"They are not so deadly a foe as minotaurs or Kottri," Karyna replied evenly.

"So I can go then, and you wouldn't worry at all?"

"Of course I would," she said quickly.

"Then I stay here with you," Aikur said with a satisfied nod. "Besides, I think the council overestimates the goblin presence. I have not seen sign of any larger forces."

"Jereth says that he saw three goblin scouts," Karyna put in.

Aikur shook his head. "Jereth is given to the drink, and that makes him see things that aren't there." Dezri turned and head-butted Aikur in the thigh, snarling and growling. Karyna laughed and stepped back, knowing all too well what was to come. "What is this? A challenger?" Aikur shouted. Dezri put up two tiny fists and looked up at Aikur with his bright, green eyes. Aikur dropped to his knees and put his fists up as well. "Well, come on then, let's see who is stronger."

"I stwonger!" Dezri shouted. The toddler then tipped his head forward and started punching as furiously as he could. Aikur grunted, making a show of flinching and swaying with each blow. He countered with a couple of wide, slow strikes that Dezri blocked before launching counter-punches that landed squarely on Aikur's cheek.

Aikur groaned and fell to the side. He closed his eyes and stuck out his tongue, letting it hang limp from his mouth as he gave one final gasp.

A moment later Dezri kicked Aikur in the stomach with his tiny, booted foot. Aikur coughed.

"You should know better by now than to let your guard down," Karyna said.

Aikur coughed again and sat up just in time as Dezri launched himself at Aikur's chest. Aikur fell to his back while carefully holding Dezri, playing along with the small child and pretending to be tackled to the ground.

"I stwonger!" Dezri shouted as he stood on his father's chest and began stomping.

"Now that is just about enough!" Karyna scolded as she swooped in and snatched Dezri off of Aikur. "That's brutal, even for a Konnon!"

"I stwongeerrrrrr!" Dezri shouted at the top of his lungs, shaking his little fists and snarling at the sky.

"Well come along, strong one, it's time for your bath."

Aikur chuckled and propped himself up on his elbows as he watched them disappear into the large wooden house that he had purchased while Karyna was still with child.

"Yep," he said. "This is where I belong." He got up and dusted himself off. He went back to the wood pile and picked up his axe, a long-handled, double-bladed axe that had as yet chopped through more minotaurs and Kottri than wood. Aikur hoisted the retired weapon up and brought it down with one hand on the large section of wood, splitting it effortlessly.

Ka-thunk!

The next piece virtually exploded apart as the axe tore through it.

Aikur spent the next hour chopping up enough wood to last for several weeks, and then he stuck the axe into the chopping block and went to work stacking the newly cut pieces next to the house. He found the work relaxing. It wasn't much of a workout for his muscles, which were accustomed to far more rigorous regimens, but it was good for his mind, giving him time to ponder.

He had only just placed the last bit of wood on the stack when he heard the sound of horse hooves coming up the way toward his house. His first instinct was to grab his sword, and he had to remind himself that hooves no longer meant minotaurs. He made two fists and closed his eyes as he took three quick breaths. Acclimating to this life was harder than he had anticipated.

He turned to see Nolan, a tall man who lived about a mile to the west in a cabin of his own.

"Missed you at the council," Nolan said with a wave.

"Have you seen any sign of goblins?" Aikur asked. "I haven't."

"They're crafty devils," Nolan said as he pulled up on the reins and dismounted. He gave his horse a quick pat on the side, signaling to the animal that it was free to graze. Nolan then removed his gloves and stuffed them under his belt as he closed the last several yards to the stone half wall surrounding Aikur's lands. "This certainly won't keep anything out," Nolan said with a gesture toward the wall.

Aikur laughed. "It's meant only to keep Dezri in," he replied. "There is nothing in these forests that Karyna and I can't handle."

"I have three more dead sheep," Nolan said as he turned and sat on the stone wall. "Something came last night and ripped them up bad. Only ate a bit of the meat, left the rest to rot, the green devils."

Aikur nodded and moved to sit next to Nolan. "Goblins aren't the only things that might do that. I have seen wolves do the same."

"Bah, wolves around here don't act like that. They only take what they can eat."

Aikur shrugged. "In New Konnland, the wolves had more than enough to eat. They still hunted our livestock though, usually ripped it up, ate a couple parts, and then left the rest."

"This isn't the work of wolves," Nolan said as he fished around in a pouch for something. After a moment he came up with the front half of a wooden arrow. "You know any wolves that use stone arrowheads?"

Aikur smiled. "All right, so if there are goblins, why not send for the town guard?"

"The town guard?" Nolan huffed. "I thought you were a Konnon! I can't believe you would suggest asking someone else to fight our battles for us."

"Lord Consuert has responsibility for the mountains. My responsibility is to my family. If the goblins come here, then sure, I'll fight, and so will my wife, but I am not about to leave them behind and go off into the mountains searching for enemies who are barely more dangerous than a pack of teenagers."

Nolan puffed air and tossed the broken arrow at Aikur. "A pack of teenagers huh?"

"Where I come from, children start training at the age of three. Those who can't master their weapons by the age of seven are assigned to trades. By the time a male is thirteen, he is more deadly than any goblin from these mountains." Aikur waved his hand toward the verdant peaks rising in the distance. "The goblins out here are small, weak, and cowardly. They won't ever come down into this area."

"A house dog may be docile and cuddly," Nolan remarked, "but throw it out into the wild and it will turn savage. One dog on its own may not pose a threat, but put it into a pack and you have the makings of trouble. We are not on New Konnland, and our children are not the brave fighters of your homeland."

Aikur shook his head. "A pack of dogs is easily run off by the town guard," he maintained. "My fighting days are behind me. I built this home. I organized the gardens. My concern now is giving my family a better life than we would have had. If I leave them now for more wars, I will have failed."

Nolan smiled and shook his head. "Won't you at least return to town with me? They're having another council later on today."

"I don't see much point in sitting around and discussing things that may or may not become problems."

"You're a stubborn man, Aikur."

"Perhaps, but at least I know what I want."

"Oh, I don't think anyone ever met a Konnon who didn't know what they wanted. You're a stubborn race, the lot of you, but you have honor too, that I can't deny." Nolan leaned closer to Aikur and held out his hand. "I'd feel better if you would at least come to the council meeting. It will do good to see men of strong character there."

Aikur shrugged. "I have work to do here," he said. He reached out and gripped Nolan's hand firmly.

"If the goblins come here, tell me you will at least pick up a sword and fight," Nolan pressed, his worried eyes searching Aikur's face for some affirmation of hope.

Aikur laughed, his eyes twinkling as his grin spread across his dark face. "If the goblins come to my home, I will squash the lot of them with my own two hands, I assure you."

Nolan nodded and departed the property without another word.

Aikur turned back to his home and went inside. He found his wife inside, with his formal uniform in her arms. "What are you doing?" Aikur asked as he closed the door behind himself.

"I thought I should bring this out and iron it for your meeting," she said with a smile.

"I'm not going," Aikur replied as he rushed forward and blocked her path. Smiling, he reached out and took the clothes away from her. "I'm not wearing these ever again."

"Aikur, we are Konnon, war is in our blood." She looked up at him with her dark, chocolate-colored eyes and gently caressed his cheek with her hand. "Go, see what the town needs."

Aikur reached up and took her hand in his. "No, I swore we would find peace. We traveled thousands of miles to make our new life here. I can't throw away what we are building. Even if I could, they don't seek only to defend their homes. I think they mean to send an offensive force into the mountains, and you know that is not our way. Konnons only fight to protect themselves and their homes. We don't invade lands that are not ours."

Karyna stretched up onto her tip-toes and kissed her husband passionately. Karyna then took in a breath and leaned her head on his chest. "Then don't fight. Advise the others. Teach them how to fight, and how to scout. Then no one can say we refused to help, and you will not have broken your promise."

"Karyna…"

She stepped back and put a finger to his lips. "Go, and since you have taken the clothes from me, you can iron them yourself. The village council expects a Konnon warrior, and you should dress to impress." She turned away and started back through the house. "I will start preparing our next meal."

"They don't need my help," Aikur said, but Karyna wasn't listening. He smiled and watched her hips sway with each step. When at last she had disappeared from view, Aikur decided to search for the iron. There was no use in arguing with Karyna. No matter how many minotaurs or Kottri he had slain in battle, he had never quite learned the strategy for winning a disagreement with her. She was always right, as she was oft to remind him throughout their marriage.

Chapter 2

Aikur hadn't worn his uniform since before he had made the decision to leave New Konnland. He sighed now and his heart felt heavy in his chest at the thought. There was no way he could make the villagers here understand him. They were not Konnon. They did not know the value placed upon one's honor, nor the shame and disgrace heaped upon him by his family and tribe when he made the announcement that he was leaving them all behind. His departure had no precedent – no other Konnon before him had ever even considered it as far as he knew - and likely wouldn't be understood or imitated by any Konnon after. His titles and commendations had been stripped from him, and his family had disowned him, spitting upon him and cursing him and his progeny for generations to come.

Such was the Konnon way when a warrior turned his back on his duties.

Aikur was born to fight, as were all Konnons, both male and female. He had mastered his weapons well, and proven himself worthy to be the first officer of his peers. He had led countless engagements against the minotaurs in their never-ending struggle for control of the northern half of New Konnland. Yet, all of that was remembered no more by his father, or the tribe he had abandoned. Because he chose to leave, instead of remaining in New Konnland until he was too old to fight, he was an outcast. If he were to ever return to New Konnland, his own people would attack him.

It was this pain more than anything else that made Aikur so determined never to fight again. Should he pick up his weapons now, it would make a mockery of his sacrifice. Even looking at his formal uniform filled him with shame. His heart delighted to know that he had saved Dezri from a life of strife and grief, but the cost had been nearly more than he could bear.

If only the foolish villagers could understand!

Aikur forced himself to pull on his tan trousers and then slip his feet into his minotaur-leather boots. He laced them tightly and then pulled his red tunic over his muscular, and scarred, torso. Last came a jerkin made from the skin of a crocodile he had hunted himself upon turning twelve. A necklace of crocodile teeth hung around his neck and a bracelet made of Kottri claws adorned his left wrist.

"Why not wear the cloak?" Karyna asked as she approached from behind.

Aikur turned to glance at the coat and sighed. "I am not a commander anymore," he said. "I cannot put the coat on without dishonoring myself."

"We are well beyond the point of worrying about honor," Karyna said. She reached down and took the coat in hand. "Did you not kill the Kottri whose skin this was?"

"I did," Aikur said. He looked at the coat of fur with its crimson stripes set against a field of black. He remembered that fight well. This particular Kottri had been the chief of his war band, and a formidable foe. Aikur's spear had broken in the battle and he had been forced to face off against the three hundred pound cat-man with his dagger. Aikur still bore the scars from this Kottri's claws. "Still, I am without title now, and therefore I should not wear it."

"Put it on," Karyna said. "The people want to be reassured that a master warrior has their backs in case the town guard fails to stop the goblin threat."

"Goblins, what goblins?" Aikur asked. "I have scouted around the property and seen no sign of any goblins. I'm sure it is just their overactive imaginations running away with them. At worst it is a pack of wolves, that's what I told Nolan."

Karyna held up the coat and waited, arching one of her brows and pursing her lips just enough to let Aikur know she wouldn't wait patiently for long.

Reluctantly, Aikur moved backward and allowed her to drape the cloak over his shoulders. Her nimble hands reached around and fastened the clasp in the front and then she slipped her hands down to hug him from behind.

"There, now you look like a proper warrior."

Aikur shook his head. "I *feel* like an imposter."

Karyna backed away and playfully slapped his behind. "Your tribe may say you have no honor, but they can't take away the things you *did*. Now, get out there and show those villagers what a Konnon warrior looks like."

"Why aren't *you* coming?" Aikur shot back. "You have just as many accomplishments as I do."

"No, you're wrong," she said with a wink. "I have more."

"That only proves my point. You should be the one to lead them."

Karyna shook her head. "That is not their way. In New Konnland I can lead, but not here. In this land, the males fight and the females make homes."

"That is not a sentiment I share," Aikur replied evenly.

"It's better this way. No one wants to take orders from a female, especially a pregnant one."

Aikur opened his mouth and was about to reply when his words caught in his throat and he just stood there, stunned. After blinking a few times he was able to bring himself back to his senses. "Pregnant?" he asked.

Karyna smiled.

"How long have you known?"

"A few weeks now," Karyna said.

"Why haven't you told me?"

"I just did," she said impatiently. "Now go on, get down to the village and then hurry back to me. We can celebrate properly once you have returned."

Aikur kissed his wife and then dropped to a knee so he could kiss her stomach. The proud man exited the house grinning ear to ear, eager to get this boring business over with so he could get back to his beloved Karyna.

The walk into the village took a couple hours, but it was a pleasant journey along the gently sloping mountain road flanked by tall pines on either side. Early spring brought with it blooming flowers, fluttering butterflies, and chirping birds darting through the air. It was a wonderful time made all the better by the knowledge that he was going to have another child. It had taken them a long time to have Dezri, longer than most Konnon couples, and Aikur hadn't been sure they would be able to make another baby, but he was walking with a great bounce in his step just thinking about his new child.

When he arrived at the village, two men armed with spears looked up and waved at him. He nodded to them and walked past. By the looks of their clothes, they were new trainees inducted into the town guard, or perhaps mercenaries hired by Lord Consuert. Mercenaries were a strange lot to Aikur. Though he understood better than most on this continent what it meant to make a living by fighting wars, he could not see the honor in hiring out to fight *others'* wars. In New Konnland, survival of both the individual and the tribe depended upon valiant warriors, but such was not the case for a mercenary. All they stood to lose by living in peace was a few coins here and there that could likely just as easily be earned working in one of the larger cities.

Though his people certainly had money and a bustling economic system, Aikur couldn't bring himself to understand the love of gold that held so many people captive in this land.

He continued along the road as it curved past a couple of sloped fields and then around a large farm house before coming into the heart of the village. A few shops and houses were built close together, and a church stood in the center of the settlement with a tall bell tower that served to remind people when to worship, and also to warn them of danger. Behind the church was a small graveyard, and behind that was a longhouse which was used as the town hall. Aikur moved to the building and pushed the door open to find roughly twenty men seated on either side of a long, rectangular table. Whatever they had been saying before he arrived was banished from each set of lips, and the group fell silent as they looked up. There were several wide-eyed expressions, and more than a couple mouths hanging open as they stared at him.

At the head of the table was Wallace, the town master. He stood and beckoned for Aikur to come inside.

"We have been hoping you would come," he said.

Nolan reached to the empty chair next to him and slid it backward for Aikur. The large Konnon warrior nodded and went to the seat next to his friend.

"Does this mean you reconsidered?" Nolan whispered.

"My wife thought I should come, that's all, but I am not fighting."

Nolan wrinkled his nose and sighed as he straightened in his seat. "She's clever, your Karyna. She might be able to convince you where I have failed."

"Not likely," Aikur replied.

Wallace cleared his throat and looked at Aikur. "Have you come to join our warriors?"

If the room was silent when he had walked in, it was near deathly now. Aikur could hear nothing but the beat of his own heart as it seemed everyone was holding their breath.

"As I have said in the past, my fighting days are behind me," Aikur replied.

"Aren't you the same man that slew three minotaurs singlehandedly when you had a broken leg?" Krip asked.

Aikur nodded. "That was a long time ago," he started to say when someone else spoke up.

"I thought all Konnons relished war, and would fight at the drop of a hat."

Aikur sighed. "Not quite. We are renowned fighters, but that is because we live in an area that demands it of us."

"Well the goblins here demand it now," Frebir spoke up. "You can't just wish for goblins to go away. You have to show them the sharp end of a sword."

"I have scouted the woods around my house, and I haven't found any sign of goblins," Aikur cut in. "I don't see a need to fight."

"A *need?*" Dremmond echoed sarcastically. "I have seven dead cows that would disagree with you. How am I supposed to provide for my family when my livestock are slaughtered and mangled?"

"Listen," Wallace interjected. "We all look up to you, Aikur. You come from a land that is legend-worthy in our eyes. Each of us, even though we are far from the larger cities, has heard of the great Konnon warriors. My own father used to tell stories of one that was called Stonefist, and even now that history astounds me. Surely you can understand why we are eager to have you fight alongside us as we march deeper into the mountains."

Aikur sighed. "I'm sorry to disappoint you, but I cannot start a war."

A chorus of shouts cut the reverent air in the room.

"We need you!" Burren called out as he slapped the table.

"No we don't, let him be," Callen remarked.

"I don't even know if there are any goblins anyhow," Lanker put in.

Nolan folded his arms as the shouting grew loud enough that no one could be heard clearly. He cast a sidelong look to Aikur and arched a brow. "Now see what you've done?" he asked.

Aikur smiled, slightly amused at how disorderly the meeting was. Such chaos would never have been tolerated in the home of a Konnon warrior, much less during one of their council meetings.

After a few unsuccessful attempts to shout over the group, Wallace grabbed a large, spherical stone and clacked it down onto a stone plate. It took a few seconds, but the shouting died down and the men gave their attention back to the town master.

"We have not the time to quarrel amongst ourselves," Wallace announced. "I have received notice that the farmers in Jeriston have been attacked by goblins."

"Jeriston?" Aikur asked Nolan in a whisper.

"It's a town about seventy miles south of here, nestled squarely in the mountains, as we are. They raise sheep there mostly."

"Something to share with the group?" Wallace called out.

Nolan waved a hand and shook his head. "Just telling Aikur where Jeriston is located."

"No doubt the great Konnon warrior should write to them so they know not to expect his help," Grais said from across the table as he glowered at Aikur. Grais was a hard man, a little older than Aikur, with streaks of gray starting to win the war atop his scalp as the hard wrinkles around his eyes seemingly grew deeper with each day's passing. Aikur wasn't sure why Grais didn't like him, but the reason didn't matter much in the great scheme of things. The Konnon

35

warrior ignored the man's comments and kept his eyes fixed on Wallace.

Wallace said, "Grais, refrain from such outbursts, or leave. Aikur is a free man, fully capable and able to decide his own fate."

"But that's just it, isn't it?" Grais fired back. "He isn't deciding just his own fate. We all know what Konnons can do. He is worth five of any of us, and he would be a great ally, but he won't fight with us. He's a coward."

Aikur burst up from his chair so quickly that his seat toppled over behind him and skidded across the floor several inches. "I will not be spoken to like that by you, Grais," Aikur snarled. "I am Aikur Anarin, fourth son of Arays Anarin, and leader of the Fourth House of Ger'dul. I have led countless battles and not ever suffered a single defeat." Aikur gripped the handle of his dagger and ripped it free of its sheath. "I will not fight, because my honor demands that I work for peace! I made a promise to my wife before we left, before we were..." The proper word here would be *shunned*, but he couldn't bring himself to say it. "Before we departed from my people and all that we held dear, I swore to her that I would build a life much better for her and for our children. Now, if goblins come down from the mountains and look for a fight, then I shall give them one, but for now I have seen no evidence of goblins invading our lands. You are blind dogs, scared of the noises you hear and do not understand, so you assume the worst and panic." Aikur stabbed the knife into the table between them and glared into Grais' eyes. "If you think me a coward, then take up my knife and attack me. I think you will find that I will not run from a direct challenge."

There was a moment of silence as Grais looked from the knife to Aikur, and then back to the knife.

Finally, Grais rose from his seat and spat on the floor before turning to walk toward the door.

"One more thing," Aikur called out.

Grais stopped in his tracks and turned his head to look sideways over his shoulder.

"I am worth a hundred of you, not five," Aikur said.

Grais flung the door open and slammed it behind him.

Aikur wriggled the knife free from the table and sheathed it before gathering his chair from the ground and sitting down once more.

"Well," Wallace said after a moment. "If that is how you handle those who simply insult you verbally, I dare say you would stop an army of goblins should they ever come as far down as your home."

A few nervous laughs helped cut the tension.

Aikur smiled and offered a nod to Wallace. "As I said, should they come to us, I will fight. It is pre-emptively attacking them beyond the reach of our borders that I disagree with."

Wallace tapped his fingers on the table and leaned back into his chair. "Well, that is something, I suppose."

"And what are we to do until then?" Dremmond asked. "Shall we wait for more attacks until there is a proper invasion force?"

Aikur shook his head. "My wife suggested that I might serve in an advisory capacity."

Dremmond threw his hands in the air and puffed air before starting to stand up.

Wallace held up a hand. "Dremmond, sit down," the town master said. "What kind of advisory capacity?"

Aikur shrugged. "I can help train your men, and I can look at the defensive measures put in place around the village." He stopped and leaned forward so he could look at Dremmond. "I can come to your home and help you put a few things into place that would stop anything, goblin or otherwise, from predating upon your livestock."

Dremmond's eyes softened and he gave a short nod. "I'd appreciate that."

Aikur smiled. "That's why I came," he said. "I am happy to do what I can to bolster our defenses. I think you will find me quite knowledgeable in that area, and I will be able to help each of you secure your homes and your families."

"Then it is settled," Wallace said. "We will assemble the new recruits as we were discussing before your arrival, Aikur, and get them started with their training. In the meantime, if you will see to shoring up our defenses, that will greatly help to assuage the sense of worry gripping our little village."

"I may need to ask for materials," Aikur said.

Wallace nodded. "Well, if it is reasonable, then have each homeowner see to their own materials. However, if something is vital and beyond a person's reach to obtain, then come to me and the town will figure out how to acquire the necessary items."

Aikur nodded. "Very good."

"Looks like you are back in command after all," Nolan whispered.

Aikur let the comment roll off of him, but he had to admit, it felt good to be useful again.

Chapter 3

"That should do it," Aikur said as he pulled on the post one last time to ensure it was secure in the ground.

"That's it?" Dremmond asked. "A few trip wires and fencing will keep out goblins?"

"It isn't just a fence," Aikur said. The wire on the fence is a tension system. Any animal, or goblin, breaks it, and the spikes we set before will be triggered. They'll come up and slam into the intruder, giving a quick and clean death." Aikur mimicked the motion by slamming his fist into his chest. "If it's good enough for the Kottri, it will handle goblins with ease."

Dremmond chewed on a wad of tobacco leaves and then spat a small amount of brown liquid from his mouth before nodding. "I suppose it will have to do."

Aikur laughed. "Ever the skeptic," he said. "Just make sure your kids don't come and play out this way. The fence will work regardless of who triggers it."

"Jaydeen knows better than to mess with your contraptions," Dremmond said. "She's fifteen after all."

Aikur nodded. "I need to head back into town and check on the recruits."

"Very good." Dremmond turned and spat again. "Oh, before I forget. My wife baked you a shepherd's pie. She wanted to show her thanks for your help. Since you have been working with us, we haven't lost a single cow."

Aikur smiled and waved the idea off. "I don't need payment, I am glad to help if it eases her worry. Go ahead and eat the pie yourself."

39

Dremmond laughed. "I already did," he said with a wink. "I just thought I should let you know she had meant it for you."

Aikur pointed to Dremmond's tools. "I'll leave those here for you." They bid their farewells and then Aikur departed through the forests around Dremmond's pastures before turning westward for the town. He took a deep breath of the pine-scented air and smiled. Everything had gone well in the three weeks since the council meeting. Grais still gave him the stink eye, but even that old codger admitted that Aikur had done wonders to strengthen the town's defenses. Dremmond's farm was the last one to be upgraded. Now that it was done, neither goblin nor wolf would be getting in.

The large warrior found the new recruits training in a clearing a mile outside of town, using wooden poles as they dueled with each other. Leading them was Krip, the town guard captain. From what Aikur knew, Krip was a veteran that had served in the imperial army under Lord Consuert's direct command. Though, if he understood correctly, Krip had only ever been in one battle, and that was east of the mountains that marked the edge of Kelsendale and separated it from the deserts beyond. Still, Krip was a level-headed soldier for the most part, even if his experience wasn't as extensive as Aikur's.

Twenty men stood facing Krip in four neat columns five recruits deep. When Krip gave a shout, they would step forward and strike at imaginary foes with their training weapons before returning to their original stance and waiting to repeat the drill.

Aikur sighed and shook his head. He was still far from convinced of any goblin threat, but he couldn't bear to see training wasted in such a useless, monotonous exercise. He approached the group and removed his shirt, revealing a set of rippling, black muscles that stretched his skin to its limits.

"Aikur, nice of you to join us today," Krip said as he called a halt to the training exercise. "How goes the fence building?"

A couple recruits snickered, but most kept silent. Aikur noted those who had laughed and approached Krip with a proposal. "I wondered if I might show the men something?" he asked. "I know I haven't been able to spend much time here, but I thought I might impart a little to them."

"We are nearly done with their training," Krip said. "Another two weeks and each of these men will be ready to face off against goblins or any other threat that comes knocking."

Aikur glanced to the men and nodded. "Good, then how about I pick seven of them for an exercise?"

Krip hesitated. "Well, I'm not sure the men will…"

"Unless you don't think they are ready," Aikur added.

"I'm ready!" one of the men shouted.

Aikur smiled when he saw that it was one of the recruits that had laughed at him. "Good, come forward." Aikur pointed to another. "You come as well." He then continued pointing out and calling recruits up until he had all seven that had laughed. "Krip is right, I have been busy building fences while you have been learning to fight. Still, I wager a gold piece each that I can take all of you in a fair fight."

"Aikur, perhaps this is unnecessary," Krip said as he stepped in closer.

"If your men can't take on one man, then they have no business defending the town against, how did you say it? Any threat that comes knocking…"

The seven men grouped in front of Aikur and tossed their weapons to the ground.

"What are you doing?" Aikur shouted. "I said I wanted a fair fight, pick up your weapons, all of you!"

"Aikur…" Krip began.

Aikur turned to the veteran and smiled. "You might want to step back." Aikur waited until each recruit had gathered his weapon and then he motioned for them to circle around him. "Surround me, and then whenever you are ready, attack me. Do not come one at a time, however, you must make this like a real battle. Come at me all together, and show me what you can do with those sticks of yours."

The recruits looked at each other and then began laughing.

"You can't be serious," one of them said. "We'll kill you."

Aikur smiled back and shrugged. "You just keep that gold piece in mind. If you win, you get a prize."

"All right, let's do this," another one said.

Aikur shook out his shoulders and flexed his fingers. He took in a breath, steadying his nerves and calming the surge of adrenaline threatening to spike his efforts beyond what they needed to be. He wanted to teach them a lesson, but he didn't need any of them seriously hurt.

The tall warrior waited until someone on his right charged in.

A less experienced fighter may have moved immediately to counter the attacker, but not Aikur. He waited a half second longer, until the recruit was swinging his staff and others were joining in, then he broke out to the left. The staff whiffed through the air where Aikur had been standing, but the recruit had put so much effort into it that he spun round and struck one of his comrade's in the chest, knocking the man down. Meanwhile, Aikur reached up and

42

stopped a downward chop from a recruit on his left, seizing the recruit's wrist with his left hand before pivoting and bringing a knee up to slam the recruit in the chest.

Two down on the ground, and he had only made contact with one.

A recruit jabbed toward his chest, but Aikur spun away, grabbed the end of the shaft, and yanked the recruit off balance, blocking off the first attacker who had now recovered from knocking out his comrade and was back in the fight.

Aikur dropped his left elbow down onto the recruit in front of him, landing a solid blow to the base of the recruit's neck. A half second later Aikur slammed his knee into the recruit's face.

Three down.

Another recruit came in wild with a wide swing that only barely missed another recruit's head as it arced toward Aikur's face. Reflexes took over. Aikur put his left arm up, his forearm moving into a shielding position while his right hand shot out to attack the staff with a palm strike. The weapon snapped as Aikur's battle-hardened hand connected with the wood. Aikur moved like lightning, wrapping his fingers around the broken piece and flipping it upright to wield like a club. He moved his club up as if to strike, but just as the recruit lifted what was left of his weapon, Aikur launched a front kick to the recruit's solar plexus that knocked the wind out of him and left him heaving and gasping for breath on the ground.

Four down.

"YAAAAAAH!" a recruit shouted from behind.

Aikur dropped the broken shaft and lashed out with a donkey kick that caught the fifth assailant in the stomach. To the recruit's credit, he only doubled over for a moment before recomposing himself and charging in once more. Aikur spun around, connecting with a back-fist with his right hand to the recruit's jaw and then landing a solid left cross to the man's face. The recruit dropped like a sack of manure.

"That's six," Aikur said aloud as he turned to the final recruit.

"I quit!" the recruit said as he threw down his staff.

Aikur felt his blood boil. Where he came from, quitting was not an option. Surrender inevitably meant death. Before he realized what he was doing, Aikur lunged forward and grabbed the recruit by the collar, yanking him close so that they were nose to nose. "You can't quit you spineless vulc-wyrm! You surrender, you die!" He let go with his right hand and poked the recruit in the forehead. "Boom! Arrow to the face. You're dead." He then dragged the side of his hand along the recruit's neck. "Sword to the neck, you're dead!" His left hand released the recruit's collar and then latched onto the man's neck. He didn't squeeze the throat, however. Instead, he used the tips of his fingers and thumb to mimic a Kottri's teeth. "Snap! Fangs to the neck. You're dead!" Aikur then shoved the recruit onto the ground.

"Aikur…" Krip said from a few yards away.

The large warrior could feel his heart pounding in his chest. "These six are fine. Give them a few more weeks and we can test them again," he said motioning to the others on the ground. "But this one, throw him back into the pond and fish for another recruit. He's useless."

"Aikur, we work with what we have," Krip said. "I can get him ready."

"You can't train someone to grow a spine. They either have one, or they don't." Aikur then turned to the others that had been watching. "The rest of you had better take a good look. I was unarmed. If you are ever called to fight in a real battle, you had better be ready to fight dirty, and fight hard. If this had been real, I would be the only one still breathing."

"Lucas, get these men cleaned up and then go back for chow. We'll do some additional exercises afterward," Krip ordered.

"Yes sir!" one of the recruits, presumably Lucas, shouted before grabbing a couple others to help him.

"Well, at least we know one thing," Krip said calmly as he walked up to Aikur and handed the warrior his shirt.

Aikur took his clothes and gave Krip a questioning look.

"You're definitely worth more than any five of us," Krip said with a wink.

Aikur smirked and pulled his shirt over his head. "Before you berate me for being too hard on them, I can assure you that I was being as gentle as I would with any group of ten year olds back on New Konnland."

"I don't doubt it," Krip commented. "Walk with me," he said as he gestured back toward the road. "I have had a visit from one of Lord Consuert's officers. Marsten, I think his name was. Captain Marsten, to be precise."

"What did he have to say?" Aikur asked.

"Oh, just updating me on the reports, that's all. He admired your defensive work, but said that it wasn't enough."

"Has Captain Marsten ever fought minotaurs?" Aikur cut in. "My traps stop them dead in their tracks."

Krip nodded and clasped his hands behind his back. "I like you," Krip said. "You don't ever feel the need to temper your feelings or thoughts. It's refreshing."

"It's just honest," Aikur replied evenly.

"Let me be equally honest," Krip said. The two stopped and Krip sighed before clearing his throat. "Look, Captain Marsten reported that Jeriston has been sacked. There were only a handful of survivors."

"And he said goblins were responsible?" Aikur asked.

Krip nodded. "Jeriston is seventy miles south of here, so it is possible that even though you haven't seen any sign of goblins, they might very well be marching into our lands. We must act."

"How many guards did Jeriston have?" Aikur asked.

"Maybe a dozen, two dozen at the most," Krip replied. "There was a bad flu about ten years ago that took out most of the young folk in the town. Those that remained were too old to do much fighting now. Captain Marsten said they found a good number of goblin bodies, but in the end Jeriston fell."

"We have nearly four times as many guards," Aikur commented. "We also have outer defenses. We have armed our women with crossbows and fortified the town church as well. We will not fall like Jeriston."

"That isn't the point," Krip said. "Lord Consuert has ordered all able-bodied men to join in the offensive. Captain Marsten will return in one week to collect those of us who can fight, fold them into his regiment, and then set off into the mountains after the goblins."

"All of us?" Aikur asked.

"Lord Consuert feels a decisive strike is best." Krip slammed a fist into an open palm. "Crush the enemy before they can reach our town."

"Did Marsten say where the goblins were?"

Krip nodded. "He has a group of scouts watching them. The goblins are making their way north. Since they ravaged all the livestock in Jeriston, they will likely strike us next. Captain Marsten plans to rendezvous with us, and then head south by southeast and hit the enemy army head on."

"I can't go," Aikur said.

Krip looked up at him and shook his head. "With all due respect, you can't refuse. Lord Consuert is ordering all of us into the action. It might have been acceptable for you to run around avoiding your duty when there was no sign of goblins but—"

"Avoiding my duty?" Aikur cut in. "My family is my duty. I don't owe you anything! I came here for peace."

"Then you should have bloody well stayed back in Four Corners, or Rifley, or even Kildrin," Krip snapped. "This is the wilderness out here. The edge of civilization, understand? Out here we have to protect what we build, or someone else will come and take it."

"I refuse!" Aikur shouted. "I have been out on the farms. I have not seen any sign of goblins anywhere. Perhaps there is a rogue band of the little creatures, but if there is, then they are small in number. We stay inside the defenses I helped build, and we will be fine."

"Aikur, you have to be reasonable," Krip said.

"I am." The large man pointed back to the clearing where he had trounced the recruits. "You think I was hard on them? My wife would have challenged all of them at the same time, and she would have broken a few of their bones too. Any goblin foolish enough to come through the traps and fences will be stopped at my door. I guarantee it."

"So you would let the rest of the countryside burn so long as the fighting doesn't come to your door, is that it?" Krip folded his arms and kicked at the dirt. "I thought you prized your honor above all else, where is the honor in letting others suffer when you have the ability to help them?"

"Fine, I'll go to Jeriston and look around. If I see for myself that that goblins razed the whole town, then I will personally lead a defensive contingent here to protect our homes while you and Captain Marsten go out looking for the goblins."

"There isn't any time for that," Krip said. "We have to go out and find the goblins right now!"

"But don't you see? That's my point, why do we have to invade *their* lands? We can easily protect ours without doing that. Let Captain Marsten station his troops along our border. I'll even let them stay at my house, as my home is the closest to the border."

"What was that speech about having a spine back with the recruits?" Krip snipped.

"I promised my wife I would never again fight in a war. I can't break that promise unless there is no other choice. Forgive me, but until every option is exhausted, I cannot help you in the way you ask." Aikur turned and took two steps before Krip called out for him.

"Aikur, hold where you are," Krip ordered. "As captain of the town guard, I have been entrusted with the task of enforcing Lord Consuert's orders. If anyone refuses to join the fighting, then I am under orders to arrest them."

"You would arrest me?" Aikur asked, turning around and narrowing his eyes on Krip.

"Would your honor allow you to resist arrest if I was under orders to take you in for refusing to fight?"

"This is madness."

"Please, don't do this. I would much rather have you at my side then in a cell waiting for Captain Marsten to return."

"Then wait until Marsten comes back. I'll talk with him then," Aikur said.

Krip shook his head. "I can't do that. If I treat you differently, none of the town guardsmen will respect me anymore, and if we are to fight, then I need their respect and loyalty. Aikur, this is it. Either you are choosing to fight with us, or I have to take you in and put you in the holding cell to await Captain Marsten's return. The only person who can show you any lenience is Wallace."

Aikur couldn't believe his ears. He could understand Krip's position, but it seemed entirely unnecessary. There was no need for such alarm. "Very well, let's sort this out with Wallace." Aikur paused and then added, "But you aren't binding my hands or leading me by the arm."

Krip sighed and gave a nod. "Fair enough."

Chapter 4

As the two passed by the church on their way to the town hall, Aikur could have sworn he noticed someone watching him out of the corner of his eye, but when he turned to look at the window in the front of the church, the figure was gone.

"Did you see that?" Aikur asked.

"See what?" Krip said.

"I thought someone was in the church, and then they... never mind."

"Come on, with any luck Wallace will still be there if we hurry." They walked beside the graveyard, but Aikur couldn't shake the feeling he was being watched, so he turned back to the church several times, but no one was ever there. Finally, they reached the longhouse and pushed their way inside.

"He's still here," Krip said with a nod toward the far end of the long table in the middle of the main hall.

"Aikur! What a pleasant surprise," Wallace said. "I was just telling Paavo here about your improvements to the town." Wallace pointed to a tall man seated at his left.

Aikur nodded to the man and noted that Paavo was very obviously a soldier. He wore a dark cloak, the hood pulled back to reveal short, dark hair set over a scarred cheek and a pair of piercing blue eyes that resembled the ocean's violence more than its beauty. A pair of short swords rested on the table in front of him, and a bow was leaning against the chair beside him.

"Wallace tells me you are a legendary warrior," Paavo said. "I don't think I have ever had the pleasure of meeting one of your kind."

"My kind?" Aikur echoed, a hint of anger giving his words edge.

Paavo grinned slightly, but didn't make an attempt to apologize.

"He walloped seven of our recruits today," Krip said as he gestured for Aikur to take a seat.

"Recruits? That's a bit below your skill level, wouldn't you say?" Paavo said as he turned his right hand over to inspect his nails. "I would think that seven recruits would hardly break a sweat for you."

"I was proving a point," Aikur said. "They need to understand the realities of the battlefield."

"Quite right," Paavo said with an approving grin. "I'm sorry I missed it."

"Right, well, Wallace, we have something we need to discuss with you," Krip said.

"Ah, that's my cue to leave, I take it?" Paavo said. "No matter, I'm sure I will get plenty opportunities to see you in action. I look forward to fighting beside you, Aikur," Paavo said.

Aikur took his seat and folded his arms. "I'm not going to be joining your forces," Aikur said flatly.

Paavo's smile vanished. "A Konnon who refuses to fight?"

"Aikur, let's keep this between the three of us," Krip said, resting a hand on Aikur's shoulder.

Aikur shrugged it off. "I have seen no proof of goblins in these parts," Aikur said. "So I can't justify an invasion into their lands."

"Their lands?" Paavo scoffed. "Do you hear yourself? You would give the goblins the same rights to land and resources that we have? Preposterous. They're animals.

51

Like the minotaurs and the Kottri you Konnons are famous for fighting."

"I killed hundreds of minotaurs and Kottri," Aikur said with a nod. "But we never once invaded their territory. We kept to ourselves on New Konnland. When we arrived, the Kottri and the minotaurs only occupied a small portion of the southern region. We stayed in the north. We fight defensive wars only."

"Ah, well then perhaps you haven't been informed; Jeriston was destroyed," Paavo said as he took up his weapons and secured them around his waist. "This is a retaliation, not an invasion."

"All I have is Marsten's word, but where is the proof?" Aikur countered.

"Proof?" Paavo echoed. The man narrowed his icy blue eyes on Aikur and shook his head. "Neither your race nor your heritage will exempt you from fighting alongside us. We all must do what we can to protect that which we have built. Lord Consuert has issued orders, and we must obey them."

"Where I come from, a commander shows proof that fighting is necessary, and then they lead the charge. If the goblins are such a threat, then why does Lord Consuert sit at his home hundreds of miles away?"

"Aikur, shut your mouth," Krip whispered in the large warrior's ear, but Aikur shook his head.

"Perhaps it is true then," Paavo said. He turned to Wallace and pointed at Aikur. "I had heard rumors that this particular Konnon only came to Kelsendale because he had lost the stomach to fight."

"Show me a goblin coming here, and I will defend!" Aikur roared. "Until then, I see no reason to waste our time provoking something that may turn into a larger fight. There are goblins in the mountains, many of them, but they do not come down here. Even if a few of them did, invading the deeper reaches of the mountains will only provoke the rest of them into war. If we lead an offensive, it will become far more bloody than any of you can imagine. Have you ever seen a nation desperate to keep its homeland?"

"The mighty Konnon is afraid," Paavo stated.

"I would command a garrison if you wish, but I will not be part of an invasion. It goes against everything I stand for." Aikur turned to Wallace. "This isn't just about the promise I gave to my wife. This is about honor. No Konnon starts a war if there is any other option. We have our defenses, we are safe here. Let Captain Marsten and his army station themselves at my house. If the goblins come, we will be ready, but at least we will not become the aggressors."

"At your house?" Paavo said. "I see, so you won't fight to protect others, but you would want an entire army posted at your home to protect you, just in case. How noble."

"Enough," Wallace said. He stood up and offered a nod to Paavo. "Excuse us, and I will see if I can talk reason into Aikur's head."

"And if he proves stubborn?" Paavo asked.

"Then he will sit in the holding cell until he comes to his senses," Wallace said.

Paavo nodded. "Very well. I have orders that take me north to another small town. I will probably return with Captain Marsten." He turned to Aikur. "I hope to see you ready for battle then. I would hate to have a Konnon wasting away in a cell while the rest of us do his fighting for him."

"You did it now," Krip said as he took the seat on Aikur's right.

Paavo left the hall and closed the door hard on the way out.

"You idiot," Wallace said after Paavo had gone. "If you could have kept your mouth shut, I might have been able to work something out, but not now!"

"I had to say what I thought," Aikur replied.

"Enough! I don't care what you think. I care what Lord Consuert thinks! If I allow you to make a fool of me in front of Consuert's men, what do you think will happen here?"

Aikur started to respond, but Wallace slapped the table to quiet him.

"I'll tell you what will happen. Lord Consuert will put Captain Marsten in charge of the town. Then I won't be able to help anyone. He'll declare martial law. Everyone will have to evacuate, and those left behind will have to fight. The whole town would be turned into a war camp, and nothing would be left of it by the time this whole thing ends. Don't you see? You are forcing me to put you in a cell unless you promise to cooperate right now."

Aikur shook his head. "Everything I said was true. We are legendary warriors, but Konnons do not invade others' lands. Our strength comes from knowing that our wars are righteous - that we defend life and honor."

"Goblins have killed our livestock!" Wallace shouted. "You can't keep denying it. The proof is clear as the day is long!"

"No, all I have been shown are mutilated animals and a few stone arrowheads. Tell me, why would goblins come in and slaughter our animals, risk retaliation, and then not take the meat?" Aikur asked. "If Jeriston was destroyed, then why was most of the meat wasted there as well?" Aikur looked to Krip. "That is what you told me, is it not?"

Krip nodded. "That is how it was explained to me, but we can't expect to know what goes on in a goblin's head. They are savages. They're beasts. Nothing more."

"They have brains and walk upright as man does," Aikur said. "They understand enough to know that you don't go into a snake pit and start kicking vipers without getting bitten in return."

"Aikur, this is the way it is here," Wallace said. "We all do what Lord Consuert orders. Normally, we are left to ourselves, but in times of need, we have to rise up to face our challenges."

"How do we know it isn't a band of human brigands living in the forest?" Aikur asked. "Why goblins?"

"Why would a human mutilate cattle?" Wallace asked.

"Maybe they didn't like Lord Consuert," Aikur huffed.

Krip slapped a hand to his forehead. "Aikur... use your head for once instead of your angry heart."

"I am!" Aikur shouted. He turned back to Wallace. "Give me a week. Let me go and investigate Jeriston. Let me see what happened there."

"Why, so you can verify whether it was goblins?" Wallace asked.

Aikur nodded. "Precisely. I need proof before I can act."

Wallace sighed and leaned back in his chair. "Aikur, you have to stop. Doesn't it occur to you that maybe, just *maybe* you might be wrong? Nolan says it was goblins that attacked his homestead. Dremmond says goblins attacked his cattle. Others have reported similar instances. Captain Marsten reports that an entire town has been razed by goblins, and you are sitting in denial." The town master leaned forward and clasped his hands on the table. "I know your promises are sacred to you, but in this case, I see more than enough proof that the time has come to make an exception to your vow of peace. After all, your home is the closest to the wilderness. If the goblins attacked en masse, they would strike your home first. Surely you believe that would be good enough to justify breaking your oath, don't you?"

Aikur sighed and looked up at the ceiling. Why couldn't they see? Something wasn't right. "Have you seen one goblin body?" Aikur asked.

Wallace sighed and shook his head. "No, but that doesn't change the fact that these attacks happened. For all I know, it could be a band of ogres. They have been known to mutilate livestock and kill people, but it isn't something we can ignore."

"How many attacks have occurred since I built up our defenses?" Aikur asked.

"Zero," Krip said.

"That's right. Not one single sheep or cow has been harmed since we put up my traps. That tells me that we have done enough to ward off whatever was attacking our animals."

Wallace shook his head. "Krip, see that he is comfortable and has enough food and water."

Aikur's mouth fell open. "You aren't serious," he said.

Wallace shrugged. "You won't agree to fight with us, and I can't let Paavo report that I am too weak to control my town. Just... go quietly and we'll try to sort this out tomorrow."

Chapter 5

Aikur sat on the rickety cot, which still smelled of booze thanks to the town drunk that normally occupied the only holding cell, and lightly thumped the back of his head against the wall. Had everyone gone mad? Why were the others so quick to believe that Jeriston had in fact been attacked by goblins? Why not augment defenses here and then send a search party to investigate?

As if someone had heard his thoughts, a voice called out as the door at the top of the stairs opened up, casting a bit of light down into Aikur's darkened cell.

"Aikur, you awake?"

It was Wallace. Aikur sighed and leaned forward, hoping that a few hours had been enough to convince the town master of his errors. "I'm awake," Aikur replied.

"You have a visitor," Wallace said.

Aikur turned to see long, shapely legs descending the steps and knew instantly who had come. "Karyna," he said with a smile. He rose from his cot and moved to the old iron bars that held him prisoner.

"So, this is where you would rather spend your nights instead of sharing my bed?" Karyna teased as she approached. The flame from the ceramic oil lamp in her hand cast dancing shadows upon her right cheek, obscuring her smile just a bit.

"How did you know I was here?" Aikur asked. He slipped his fingers through the bars, reaching out for her hand. Karyna grabbed him with her free hand and sighed with a shake of her head.

"Nolan said he saw you come into town with Krip, and suggested that I should come for myself."

"Was he in the church?" Aikur asked, guessing that it had been Nolan he had seen watching him earlier.

Karyna shook her head. "No, he was in the general store trading for supplies. Why do you ask?"

Aikur shrugged. "It doesn't matter. Karyna, where is Dezri?"

"I brought him along. Nolan and Wallace are watching him upstairs."

"Ah, so they sent you to talk to me, is that it?"

Karyna nodded. "I know it is not our way, but perhaps we can change. After all, we are not in New Konnland anymore," she said.

"But I am still Konnon," Aikur replied. "I have already turned my back on my people. I won't give up what little honor I have left by invading the mountain lands."

"Why is it so important to you?" Karyna asked.

"My father, and his father before him, and his before him, they all passed down the teachings of Dossman Steeds. New Konnland was given to us as a promised land from the gods, but only if we gave up our abhorrent ways and traditions. When the minotaurs and Kottri challenged us, we had to defend ourselves, but we couldn't give in to our lust for battle. If we went beyond the borders of our promised land to seek new land through blood, then we would have rejected the new life the gods had given us."

"But we are in a different land, with different rules," Karyna said. "I know you mean well, but sometimes you can be too stubborn."

Aikur grinned. "Do I shame you, my wife?"

"No, my husband. I am not ashamed of you," Karyna replied as she reached in and stroked the side of his face with her fingers. "But think on it. We must live with these people. Perhaps there can be compromise between their ways and ours. After all, they have graciously accepted us into their culture and their lives. Should we not embrace them as well?"

"If the goblins, or any foe, were to come to the town, you know I would be out in front, defending all that we hold dear, but I cannot lead a charge into lands that are not ours. I would dishonor my fathers, and in turn I would dishonor Dossman Steeds. I may be here, among strangers, but I cannot change all that I am to suit them. I must do that which is honorable."

Karyna sighed and shook her head. "You are as thick headed as an ox, but I do love you."

Aikur smiled and tried to squeeze enough of his face through the bars to get a kiss.

Karyna moved in and gave him a quick peck on the lips and then pulled away. "I should take Dezri home." She turned away, but then stopped and looked over her left shoulder. "Aikur, think on it. See if there can't be room in your honor for their ways as well. If there are goblins out there attacking towns, would it not be honorable to bring them to justice?"

Aikur frowned, but offered a somber nod. "I will think on it," he said.

"Good, then I will be back in the morning. Get some sleep." She went up the creaking stairs and through the door. As the portal closed behind her, Aikur's cell was cast back into darkness.

He slapped one of the bars and then turned to find his cot and sit down once more. "Even my own wife thinks..." Aikur stopped mid-sentence and shook his head. "Perhaps she is right." He leaned back against the wall and took in a deep breath. "If my father were here, what would he say?" Aikur asked himself aloud. He already knew the answer. Aikur's father would be sitting in the cell right beside him, just as stubborn and adamant as he was. An offensive war was not their way.

Aikur slid off from his cot and knelt on the ground. He envisioned his father in his mind, as if the man was walking toward him from somewhere in the Plane of the Dead. "Father, give me your wisdom," Aikur prayed. He pushed all other thoughts from his mind and concentrated on the image of his father, imagining that he drew nearer. Aikur slowed his breathing. "Father, tell me what to do."

The image stood tall and proud in Aikur's mind. His father's silver hair looked almost like a crown upon his head, and the traditional cloak and robes displayed generations of Anarin family pride and honor. Aikur's father looked down at him, and smiled.

"Father," Aikur implored once more as he focused on the image in his mind. "Tell me what I should do."

Arays Anarin took in a breath, and then he turned around and walked away without saying a single word.

"Father!" Aikur called out. The image in his mind would not heed him. Soon there was only darkness in Aikur's mind, and he was left to himself. He opened his eyes and pushed up from the ground. Had his father come only to shun him? Aikur sighed heavily and walked to the far wall of his cell. "Have I dishonored you so greatly by seeking peace?" Aikur asked as if his father could hear him. "I have never felt alone before, but…" Aikur shook his head and placed his hands on the wall as he leaned into it. He hadn't prayed to his father since before leaving New Konnland.

He and Karyna had seemed so sure of their choice that neither of them felt the need to consult with their respective ancestors. They made their announcement to their tribal elders, and then boarded a ship for Kelsendale without any real amount of debate. It was the best thing to do for Dezri, of that Aikur was sure.

Or was it?

Other Konnons would grow up with one less Anarin clan to protect them. Dezri would no longer stand as a proud link in the chain of warriors that spanned generations. He would grow to be an outsider. Aikur had known all along that he would be dishonored for leaving, but this was the first time he felt regret for his decision. What was to be done? Perhaps Karyna was right. Maybe they had become something other than true Konnons. If that were true, then dishonoring Dossman Steeds' teachings was not the worst thing he could do. If even his father shunned him, and refused to accept him, then his only honor would come from how he worked with his new neighbors.

He turned around and paced back toward the bars of the cell door, shaking his head and arguing with himself between the merits of retaining what little honor he imagined himself as possessing, and merging with the people of this new town. If Nolan was to go out and fight in the mountains, then should Aikur really sit behind and do nothing?

He spent the next two hours pacing back and forth in his cell, continuing the debate.

Then, after a long struggle, an idea occurred to him, and a smile crossed his lips.

Aikur rushed to the cell door and called out. "Wallace! WALLACE!"

No answer.

"WALLACE, come down here!" Aikur shouted. Still, no answer.

Aikur grunted and wrapped his fingers around the bars. He gave it a shake and smiled when he discovered that the bolts securing the left side to the stone wall had come loose. Sure, they were strong enough to hold in an unconscious drunkard, or perhaps a young adolescent caught stealing, but there was nothing holding Aikur in the cell. The large man positioned himself near the left side of his cell and gave three solid kicks to the bars. Each strike pulled and bent the bolts until the last kick popped them loose in a shower of dust. Aikur then pushed the whole frame until the upper and lower rails that secured the bars in place bent just enough for him to squeeze through.

Aikur rushed up the stairs and grabbed the door knob. It too was locked. Aikur sighed and leveled his shoulder, preparing to knock the door open. He backed up and then charged upward, but just before he made contact the door swung open.

A wide-eyed Wallace yelped and dove out of the way as Aikur tumbled out of the doorway and onto the wooden floor of the main hall.

"Hey Wallace, I was trying to call for you," Aikur said as he rolled over to face the town master, who was pushing himself up and brushing off the front of his pajamas.

"Yes, I heard you, I just thought I would wait until morning before trying to talk with you again," Wallace said.

"Is this how you treat normal prisoners?" a voice called from the table.

Aikur turned over to see Paavo sitting there. "Hi," Aikur said with a sheepish grin and a wave. Paavo returned the greeting with a half-hearted salute. "I wasn't trying to escape," Aikur put in quickly. "I just wanted to say that I found a way that would allow me to fight with everyone else and still retain my honor."

"I see," Paavo said as he poured himself a drink from a long necked wine bottle. "And you thought busting out of the cell would prove your willingness to help, is that it?"

Aikur stood up and shrugged as he moved to the table. "The only thing holding me in that cell was my word anyhow. I could have escaped anytime I wanted to."

Wallace grunted and moved to the table as well. "Paavo, pour me a glass as well."

"I thought you had to leave?" Aikur asked as he sat down.

"I decided to wait until the morning. I wanted to see how Wallace would handle your conversation." He took a drink and then smiled. "Sending for your wife was a shrewd move," Paavo said.

"Nolan saw me come into town, he told her to look in on me, that's all," Aikur said.

"No, actually I sent him to fetch her," Wallace put in. "I had hoped she would be able to get through to you. We need your help. Most of the townsfolk don't have any real experience, and you already saw how the recruits are faring."

Aikur nodded. "I can help, but first I need to know something," the large warrior said. "I can justify attacking the goblins as an answer to their attack on Jeriston, but the borders have to stay the same. We can't claim any of the wilderness beyond our borders in battle."

"Why not?" Paavo asked pointedly. "Don't we have a right to keep what we take in war?"

Aikur shook his head. "Because my honor will not allow me to fight a war only to enlarge our borders. It is a part of me that I cannot change. But, as long as we don't do that, then I can join the expeditionary force."

"So now you believe there are goblins?" Paavo asked after another drink.

"I'm still not convinced, but my wife has helped me see that as part of this community, I should be willing to shoulder the burdens that fall upon all of us. Your ways are different from mine, but some compromise can be made."

"Excellent," Paavo said with a slap on the table. "Then I shall be happy to report to Lord Consuert that everyone has risen to the call. He will be most pleased."

Paavo turned to Wallace. "And I dare say he will remember how well you have handled the town."

Wallace tried to duck his head and hide his grin, but failed miserably. Aikur could easily see that the man was beyond pleased to hear that his name would be spoken well of to Lord Consuert.

"Well, shall we retire for the remainder of the night?" Paavo asked after draining the rest of his wine.

Wallace raised his goblet and gave a nod. "To victory over the foul, green-skinned buggers that plague our woods." He drank the entire drink and then set his goblet on the table and smacked his lips. "Aikur, it might be best for you to spend the rest of the night here. You can return home in the morning."

Aikur frowned. "No, I think I should be going."

"You'll need your sleep," Wallace countered. "Tomorrow you and Krip will be discussing who takes command over the town guard."

Aikur waved the notion away. "Let him command. I will be a good soldier when needed, but I don't need to command. Your men have trained under him, and they have a good synergy. It's best not to stir things right before a possible engagement."

"Well spoken." Paavo stood up and stuck the cork back into the bottle. "I am headed into the guest room. Sweet dreams gentlemen."

"I'm going up to my own room," Wallace said. "That leaves the cell downstairs."

Aikur glanced to the still open door leading to the cell and then back to Wallace. "You want me to sleep in there?"

Wallace tossed the key to Aikur. "In the morning I'll have you help repair whatever you did down there too. Get some rest."

Chapter 6

Aikur woke early the next morning. Unable to fix the bars he had bent out of place, he worked with the blacksmith, mostly holding things steady while the smith worked to set a new frame of bars in. When he had finished, Wallace offered him a bit of bread and cheese, but Aikur refused, anxious to leave and get back to his wife.

"I'll go with you," Paavo called out.

Aikur stopped, his hand resting on the ring of iron set into the town hall's front door. "You want to go with me? I will only take you in the wrong direction."

"True, but I want to meet this wife of yours and see what kind of magic she has."

"Magic?" Aikur echoed. "She isn't a witch."

Paavo smiled and caught up with Aikur. "And yet somehow she was able to reason with someone that had only hours before had a head seemingly made of stone." Paavo slapped Aikur on the back and stepped out ahead of him. "I'd say she's at least an enchantress."

Aikur grinned and followed after Paavo. "Perhaps there is some truth to what you say," he commented. "Without her, I may never have changed my mind."

"Exactly my point. Maybe we can send her to the goblins," Paavo said with a wide grin. "She can flash her pretty smile and dazzle them into believing they should just pack up and go to the other side of the mountains. It would save us all a lot of trouble. After all, the goblins can't be as thick-headed as you were yesterday."

Aikur snorted. "If you sent her, she would likely bring back all of their heads," he said. "She is a better fighter than I am."

"Truly?" Paavo asked. "I heard that Konnon women fought in the army, but I have never known any, so I thought it might be a rumor."

Aikur shook his head. "No, it's very true. They are cunning and ferocious. My wife's tally of slain minotaurs is higher than my own, and she has killed nearly the same number of Kottri as well."

"Could she take you in a fight?" Paavo asked.

Aikur laughed. "I should think you already know the answer to that question based upon last night."

"Ah, so her enemies she defeats with the blade, and her husband she conquers with her smile. I think I shall like her."

Aikur nodded as they walked by the church. The large warrior glanced to the windows once more, but this time there seemed to be no one inside. "Do you have a wife?" Aikur asked.

Paavo grunted. "Had one once," he said with a half-smile. "Didn't go very well."

"What happened, did she get sick?"

"You could say that," Paavo said. "She contracted a case of loneliness. Apparently, it got worse each time I left the house."

Konnor frowned. "I'm sorry."

Paavo shrugged. "It's all right. We never had any children, and sooner or later I came to realize I loved roving the wilderness more than being at home anyhow. We were both happier going our separate ways."

"I couldn't live without my Karyna," Aikur said. "We have been together since we were fourteen. Our fathers arranged the marriage after they realized they couldn't keep us apart. It has been wonderful. That's why we decided to move here. We didn't want our children to grow up only knowing the harshness of New Konnland."

Paavo nodded. "What was that like? I have never been on the seas, let alone out to New Konnland."

"It's hot, humid, and wild," Aikur said. "The soil is good, thanks to the volcanoes in the north. The ore is also plentiful for weapons and the like."

"Gold?" Paavo asked.

Aikur shook his head. "Some, but not enough to tempt most people. Besides, there are too many Kottri and minotaurs in the lower half of the island to do much exploratory mining. Our economy runs differently. Every person has a duty to contribute to the society. We have fighters, smiths, physicians, hunters, farmers, everything you would expect, but we don't use much in the way of money."

"You share everything?" Paavo asked.

Aikur nodded. "We share enough to ensure everyone has their needs met. We do have some money, with which we can buy extra things in times of surplus, or to trade with merchants that come and bring unnecessary things like jewelry or exotic clothing."

"Interesting concept," Paavo commented. He stopped then and held out a hand. "So, if you don't need money, how could you afford to buy a place here?"

Aikur shrugged. "That's why we couldn't settle in the cities farther west of here. The only land we could afford was out here. I had just enough to buy the land, and then I built the house with the materials found on the land. It took time, but it is a fine home, and I don't have to worry about minotaurs coming to knock it down."

"Minotaurs, no, but there is an army of goblins out there with the same idea," Paavo said.

"We shall see," Aikur replied. "If there are goblins looking for trouble, I will give them more than they can handle."

Paavo smiled. "It will be good to have another veteran in the unit," he said. "I was worried that Krip would be the only man worth the effort of taking along."

"If you were worried about that, then why not leave the townsfolk behind to defend the town?" Aikur asked.

"Because I am a soldier. Lord Consuert makes the orders, and I follow them. That is my lot in life."

Aikur nodded. The two continued out through the main gate and headed north from the town into the forest. "Have you fought in many battles?" Aikur asked after they had passed the turn off to Dremmond's farm.

Paavo nodded. "I have encountered my fair share of nasty things in the forest," he said. "Most of my time has been spent patrolling the borderlands. As you can imagine, I have run into a number of brigands, fugitives, and less favorable creatures. I once fought an ogre, even," Paavo said. He motioned to the two short swords hanging from his belt. "I put two arrows into the creature's chest, and then had to finish him with my blades. It was a ghastly business. They smell something horrible before you open them up, but once their blood spills out it's as if you are consumed by a fog of their stench. It really is unbearable."

Aikur laughed. "Minotaurs are like that sometimes. Not all of them, but some clans are less cleanly than others. They reek of filth and can often be smelled half a mile away, or even farther depending on how strong the wind is."

"Ugh," Paavo put in. "You know, one time I ran into an orc, and he was the filthiest—"

Aikur stopped and thunked Paavo in the chest. "Is that smoke?"

Paavo looked up and nodded.

Aikur's heart sank as the thick column of black smoke rose up above the green pines of the mountain. "It looks to be near my house," Aikur said softly.

Paavo's mouth fell open and he turned to face Aikur. "Are you certain?"

Aikur nodded and then broke into a run. Paavo quickly caught up and then kept pace with the large warrior. They ran the last three miles to the turn off to Aikur's home in just less than twenty minutes.

"Nolan!" Aikur shouted as they followed a bend in the road around a grouping of trees and found his friend's wagon overturned in the road. The two horses were slaughtered and mutilated, their legs cut off and strewn about the road. Two of the wagon wheels were broken, and the front half of the wagon had nearly broken off from the rear.

Aikur ran around to the front and found his friend face down in the dirt, pinned beneath the wagon.

"Is he alive?" Paavo asked. Paavo now had his bow out and an arrow at the ready.

Aikur reached down and lifted the wagon up and off of his friend's back. "Pull him out!" Aikur grunted.

Paavo dropped his weapons and quickly dragged Nolan out from under the wagon.

"Nolan, can you hear me?" Aikur shouted after dropping the wagon back down.

"He's gone," Paavo said. "Look at his neck." Paavo turned Nolan over to reveal a nasty gash across the front of Nolan's neck, and two broken arrow shafts protruding out from Nolan's chest. "I'm sorry," Paavo offered.

Aikur took two steps back. "No… there aren't any goblins here!" he said. Aikur then turned to look at the smoke. "Karyna!" The large warrior sprinted off down the road as fast as he could. His feet pounded the ground beneath him as he covered the last half mile to his home in just a couple of minutes. As he emerged from the thick forest and came out into the clearing well enough to see his home, he gasped and fell to his knees, skidding across the road as his mass struggled against its momentum. "No!" he muttered. His heart pounded in his chest and his lungs burned in agony. His once beautiful home was now nothing more than two blackened walls of charred wood and a smoke-stained column of stones that had once been his chimney.

"Come on, keep moving!" Paavo shouted as he passed by Aikur, bow in hand. The scout turned back and tossed one of his short swords down in front of Aikur. "Come on!"

It might have been Paavo's urgent words, or perhaps the sight of the blade landing in front of Aikur that shook him from his terror-filled stupor, but whatever it was, he now found his strength returning. He grabbed the short sword and got up, charging down the road and leaping over the short stone wall he had built with his own two hands. He saw the many arrows littering the garden, but he didn't see Karyna or Dezri.

Perhaps they survived. *Karyna would have fought them!*

Aikur launched himself into the rubble, screaming their names as he frantically kicked burned beams and boards aside, but he found nothing.

"I have something," Paavo called out from outside the rubble.

Aikur turned and ran to the scout only to find a goblin with an axe sticking out of its chest. Aikur recognized the axe, for it was his. "Karyna did this," Aikur said. He looked up toward the tree line and saw two more bodies. He rushed up and was relieved to see that they were goblins as well. Their slight chests had been slashed through with shallow cuts and then stabbed with something that made a large hole. *Her spear.* "Karyna is alive," Aikur said.

"Do you think she went after them?" Paavo asked.

Aikur turned back to the house. "She wouldn't have left Dezri unprotected." The large warrior turned to Paavo. "Search the fields, and I'll search the rest of the rubble."

Paavo nodded and started making increasingly large circles through the tall grasses while Aikur ran back to the house and searched through what had been his bedroom. The wood remains of boards and beams were too hot to touch with his hands, but he found he could kick them away with his boots or flip them with the short sword with some efficacy. Unfortunately, he didn't find anything.

Aikur left the rubble and started toward the tree line.

"I found a toy," Paavo called out. The soldier bent down and came up with a stuffed bear.

"That's Dezri's," Aikur said. "Is Dezri…" Aikur couldn't bring himself to finish the question.

"No, I just found the toy," Paavo answered. "Maybe they took the child and your wife went after them."

"Here," Aikur said as he tossed Paavo's sword back. Paavo caught it with his left hand and twirled it once before sliding into the sheath. Aikur ran back to the goblin body where his axe was stuck and wrenched the weapon free. He turned his dark eyes to the woods and felt a fire within his chest grow hotter than any other time he could remember.

"To the hells of Hammenfein with Captain Marsten; I'm going after those goblins right now." He ran northward into the trees without turning back to see whether Paavo was following. He darted between the trees as nimbly as a deer, though his footsteps were heavy and hard, snapping twigs and crunching leaves underfoot as noisily as a New Konnland bugbear. He ran for a mile, easily tracking the trail of dark blood and goblin bodies left in the forest.

She did follow them! Aikur realized. *They must have taken Dezri. That's the only reason she would have gone after them alone.* He ran as fast as he could without stumbling as the underbrush grew thicker. After twenty more minutes of running, he

71

found a goblin pinned to a tree with the front end of a spear, Karyna's spear. The back half was broken off and had been used to stab another goblin through the throat.

"Karyna!" Aikur called out.

He spun around, scanning the forest with his eyes, but he couldn't see any sign of her.

"Is she here?" Paavo asked as he caught up and bent over to catch his breath.

Aikur shook his head. "No, but that is her spear. She must have kept going. Come on!" Aikur turned northward and continued following the trail as best he could. He ran for another ten minutes, until his legs begged for rest and his lungs burned for air. Even after a couple years of living in the mountains, Aikur was still not able to run nearly as far as he could have in New Konnland with its lower altitude. The mountain incline was becoming steeper as well, which didn't help.

The large man stopped next to a large white pine and sucked in air.

Paavo caught up with him and slapped his shoulder. "I'll take a look around. It can't be much farther."

Aikur nodded. The thought of his wife out here alone, battling for the life of their son, caused his stomach to flip and tie itself in knots. If only he hadn't been so stubborn. If he hadn't argued with Krip, he would have been home with his family. He pushed thoughts of death out of his mind. Karyna would be alive, he knew it. She was a better warrior than he was, and was not about to fall victim to a bunch of goblins.

"Aikur!" Paavo shouted from a ways off.

Hearing the urgency in Paavo's call, Aikur ran on, ignoring the growing stitch in his stomach muscles. "What is it?" he asked as he came closer.

Paavo turned with his head hanging low. "I'm sorry…"

Aikur looked down to Paavo's feet and saw a tiny, brown-skinned arm that had been cut off at the elbow. The tiny fist was still clenched, as if Dezri had fought his captors.

"NO!" Aikur shouted. He rushed forward. "He can't be dead!" He bent down and scooped up the tender, soft arm and held it to his chest while his eyes frantically darted around. "I don't see any other bodies. Maybe he's just wounded. Karyna must have fought them here. There should be goblin bodies—there has to be—"

Paavo bent down and set his bow on the ground. "Aikur, it's over," he said.

Aikur looked up at the scout and his rage boiled over. The large warrior balled his left fist and socked Paavo in the nose, shattering it out to the right and splattering blood across the ground as Paavo flew backwards to land on his rump.

"They're fine!" Aikur shouted as he stood up. "Stay if you like, run back if you're afraid, but I will find them!" Aikur looked to the north and set his jaw. With his sons severed arm in his left hand and his axe in his right, he continued on. *Karyna's all right. She has to be. She has Dezri safe. She got him back. Everything will be all right.* He kept repeating the thoughts over and over in his mind as he wound his way up a narrow game trail that ascended to a small peak littered with boulders and fallen logs.

A large amount of dried blood stained a white and gray rock in front of him. On the ground next to the rock was a necklace made of leather and blue beads. Aikur bent down and dropped his axe so he could pick up the necklace. It was Karyna's, which meant the blood was likely hers as well, and there was far too much of it staining the rock and the ground.

"Karyna?" he called out, his voice cracking. He wandered around the top of the hill, looking between boulders. He couldn't bear the thought of finding either of

73

them dead, but his feet compelled him to continue searching. As he stepped over the top of a fat, half-rotten log, he saw a brown hand sticking up over a boulder in front of him.

"Karyna!" Aikur shouted. He ran around the massive boulder, hoping he had arrived in time to help her. He rounded the rock and came to a stand-still. His mouth hung open, too weak to utter a single word. His legs quivered and then he collapsed to his knees before vomiting on the ground. His heart beat faster and faster as his vision darkened and he gasped for breath, choking on his own vomit. There was nothing he could do for her, because all he found was her arm, hacked away from her body just above the shoulder joint, with a bit of scapula bone hanging along with the limb which stood on the torn end, leaning against the boulder so that the hand and fingers managed to stick out above the rock. There was no hope that anyone could have survived such a thing. Karyna was gone, and so was his little Dezri.

"NOOOOOOOOOOO!" Aikur roared at the sky.

Aikur reached out and took Karyna's arm, holding it along with Dezri's next to his heart as he fell to his side on the ground and wept openly. Paavo came around the rock some time later, but could barely utter his sympathies to Aikur when he saw what had happened.

The large warrior cried until he passed out from emotional fatigue.

When he woke, the sun was hanging low in the sky, and the forest was growing dark. He slowly sat up and looked to Paavo, who was sitting on the large boulder with his bow across his lap.

"I hit you," Aikur said.

Paavo nodded. "I'm sorry," he said.

Aikur looked to Karyna's beautiful, blood stained hand and let tears stream down his face. "Why didn't I listen?"

Paavo sighed and slid off the rock to kneel next to Aikur. He reached out and grabbed the large man by the chin, turning him so that they locked eyes. "This is not your fault," he said.

"But it is," Aikur replied. "If I had been home, if I had listened."

Paavo slapped Aikur across the face.

For a second, Aikur's anger flared and he almost reacted by punching the man again, but Paavo's stern, blue eyes stared into his and found the fire within his soul.

"You listen to me," Paavo said. "We'll go in and get the green-skinned demons that did this. It's *their* fault. You and me, we'll kill them all."

Aikur nodded.

"We will avenge your family, don't you doubt it, not even for a second."

"I will kill every last one of them," Aikur said.

Paavo then moved his right hand and poked his index finger into Aikur's chest. "You keep your family right here. In the meantime, remember, they're in a better place. They'll be waiting for you when your life is over."

Aikur looked down at Paavo's finger and shook his head. "No, they won't," Aikur said. "Konnons can't go to heaven unless last rites are performed at their burial."

Paavo scrunched up his face. "So, perform the ritual then. I can help you if you need."

Aikur shook his head and pushed Paavo back. "No, you don't understand. I need their whole bodies. I can't perform the last rites with only..." Aikur looked down to the severed body parts and the tears flowed harder than ever. "If I can't recover their bodies, then they're damned to Hammenfein."

Chapter 7

Aikur sat next to the shallow graves that held all he could find of his wife and son. He stared at the stone markers, clutching his wife's necklace in one hand and his son's stuffed toy in the other. Paavo had helped dig and bury them as he had promised, but he was quick to return to town. He had asked Aikur to come, but the large Konnon refused, opting to stay by the small graves through the night and into the following day.

A large monarch butterfly gently came down and rested upon Dezri's grave. Aikur closed his eyes as tears fell out across his cheeks.

"See Dezri, you have to be still and let them come to you," Aikur whispered. He took in a breath and reached out to lay Dezri's toy on the grave as the butterfly fluttered away. "I will see you again, soon." Aikur then moved some of the earth covering his wife's severed limb and placed her necklace into the ground. "And I will see you as well. I swear it." He choked on a lump in his throat and had to growl in order to clear it from his neck. "I will brave the fires of Hammenfein if that's what it takes, but first, I will find those that did this to you, and I will cut their heads from their bodies and build a wall on the edge of our land that shall forever warn the goblins not to set foot on Anarin land again." He bent down and kissed the stone markers, and then he got up and gathered his few belongings that had survived the fire and started walking down the road away from his house.

He was nearly to the main road when he saw Paavo, Grais, and Wallace approaching on horseback.

"Aikur!" Wallace called out as he urged his horse to move faster.

Aikur stood still and waited as they drew nearer.

"I'm so sorry," Wallace said. The town master hopped off the horse and moved in with his arms outstretched as if to embrace Aikur, but Aikur did not move to return the gesture. Wallace wrapped his arms around Aikur's shoulders. "We had no idea the goblins were so close," Wallace said as he stepped back from the large Konnon.

"Too bad your defenses didn't keep the green-skinned devils out," Grais said.

Aikur looked to Grais with fire in his eyes. "You dare make jokes?" Aikur said.

Grais held up a hand. "No, I mean it, sincerely!"

It was too late. Aikur's anger had boiled beyond containment, and it needed release. Aikur dropped his things, took two steps and punched Grais' horse in the eye. The horse turned to bolt away, but not before Aikur snatched Grais and ripped him down to the ground.

"Aikur!" Wallace shouted.

Aikur was beyond hearing. His anger was focused on Grais. He bent down and grabbed the man by the left ankle and with one quick twist he yanked Grais up from the ground and swung him off into the bushes to the side of the road.

Grais tumbled through the underbrush, grunting and crying out as he thunked against the ground and then bounced to strike the side of a tree trunk.

Paavo was in front of Aikur before the large warrior could follow his prey.

"Not like this!" Paavo said. "Save your anger for those who deserve it!"

Aikur stopped and stared at Paavo's purple nose and black eyes. In that moment he remembered striking Paavo as well. The Konnon nodded and turned to pick up his things. "I don't want to wait for Captain Marsten," he said. "I want to go ahead now."

Paavo nodded. "I have sent word to Captain Marsten," he said. "I thought you might want to do something like that. I'll go with you."

"I would be better alone," Aikur replied.

"Krip is going too," Wallace said.

"Krip needs to lead the town guard," Aikur said.

Paavo shook his head. "Wallace will keep the town guard in a defensive pattern around the town. All the outlying farms have been ordered to come into town." Paavo turned to Aikur and sighed. "You should know, Nolan's farm was destroyed as well."

"But others were spared," Wallace put in quickly.

"Keep him away from me," Aikur said with a nod to Grais, who was just pulling himself to his feet and brushing his clothes off.

"Aikur, I am truly sorry," Wallace said.

"They will be sorry too," Aikur promised. "Every last goblin I find is going to wish their maker had never given them life."

Aikur shouldered his bedroll and equipment and then moved past Wallace and Paavo.

"You can have my horse," Wallace said.

Aikur shook his head as he kept walking. "I don't know how to ride one, and I will be a better fighter on my own feet."

There was a rustling sound from behind him as Paavo removed what he needed from his saddle bags. The scout then ran to catch up with Aikur.

"What about Krip?" Paavo asked.

"If he isn't here, then he should stay with the town guard."

"He's a good soldier," Paavo said. "He can help."

Aikur ignored Paavo and quickened his pace. The two were nearly running by the time they reached the main road. Krip was waiting there, standing in his tight-fitting uniform from the days when he was a much younger man. Unlike Wallace and Paavo, Krip didn't say anything. He exchanged a somber nod with Aikur, and then fell in with the large Konnon as they turned northward.

They traveled for two miles before the road stopped, ending at a large wooden blockade with an old sign hanging on the front.

Aikur moved to the sign and read the words. "Danger, beyond this point are goblins, ogres, orcs, and other dangers." He gripped his axe, raised it high over his head, and then destroyed the barricade with one savage chop, splintering the wood to the side. "Someone should make a warning about me," he snarled.

The trio then moved through the trees, but unlike other days, Aikur did not notice the clean scent of pine, nor the happy birds chirping in the branches above. He could only hear the screams of his dying wife, and in his mind he alternated between imagining their pain and seeing his father's spirit turn his back on him. Everything was gone.

He had known many Konnons who had lost their families, but never before had he known of any whose deceased relatives had been denied final rights. Death was a harsh reality for a Konnon, but an eternity without one's family was the worst kind of hell. No threat of injury or death could be worse than the fate handed to Aikur. As he continued through the forest, his rage built up inside of him, threatening to burst from him like a volcano pushed to its utmost limits before the pressure explodes. His anger gave him strength, and quickened his feet so that he crossed many miles into the mountains over the next two hours without stopping for rest, putting him easily farther than a mile ahead of either Paavo or Krip, who were having significant trouble matching his pace.

Then, as he came over the crest of a small hillock attached to the tall mountain he was climbing, he found a group of seven goblins. They sat around a fire, eating and talking in their obscene, guttural language that Aikur couldn't understand. His legs propelled him down toward their camp site with incredible speed. As the goblins all had their backs to him, none of them saw his approach until it was too late.

Aikur brought his axe down on the goblin in the middle right as two of the creatures noticed him for the first time, jumping up from their seats and squawking loudly as they reached for swords and bows. The goblin in the middle barely had time to look up from his meal of roasted venison leg before Aikur's blade cut him from the top of the skull down through his spine and into the log he rested upon, effectively severing the goblin in two.

The few goblins nearest Aikur's first victim cried out in horror and tried to scatter away, but Aikur's rage quickened his muscles. He lashed out with a kick to his right that caught a second goblin in the middle of the back and launched it forward, stumbling toward the dying fire and skewering itself on the spit they had used for the deer.

Aikur leapt over the log and brought the shaft of his mighty battle axe up, slamming the pommel into another goblin's forehead and caving the bone in with a sick, wet *ker-klick!* Aikur then wheeled around, holding his axe parallel to the ground as he spun until he caught the fourth goblin in the chest, burying his blade so deep into the creature that it nearly broke through the spine and out the other side. As that goblin fell lifelessly to the ground. To save time, Aikur let go of his axe and rushed the next nearest goblin, who was in the process of putting an arrow to his bowstring. Aikur

80

snatched the bow with his left hand and raised it up just as the goblin fired. The bowstring stung Aikur's knuckles, but the arrow flew up and away. The large Konnon came in with a hard right punch to the goblin's gut that doubled the creature over. He then wrenched the bow free and moved to stand behind the goblin. Aikur hooked the bowstring around the front of the creature's neck and then pulled back on the bow while kicking forward with his left leg, drawing the bow back to its full extension as the goblin shrieked and tried to pull the string away from its neck. Aikur released the bow, sending the wooden part slamming into the back of the goblin's head with a resounding *–CRRRACK!*

Aikur spun around just as another goblin rushed from behind with a curved sword. Aikur sidestepped a forward thrust, then snaked his right hand up and around the attacker's wrist. As he pulled up with his right hand he shot his left hand through the goblin's forearm with a front palm strike that shattered the bones. He then easily took the curved sword and slashed the goblin's neck before turning on the seventh and final foe.

The last remaining goblin stared wide-eyed at the others and then threw its weapon down and turned to run.

"No mercy," Aikur said. He tested the sword's balance and then once he had a good feel for it he launched it through the air, whirling end over end until the point drove through the goblin's spine, right between the shoulder blades.

"Grbach!" the goblin squealed as it fell forward, writhing in pain for a few seconds until the last bits of its energy ebbed away.

Aikur turned back and pulled his axe free from the goblin corpse he had left it in. He wiped the blade and then looked to the north once more. His heart wasn't beating as quickly as it had been when he had spotted these seven, but the rage in his heart was only marginally cooled.

"Icadion's beard man, can't you leave any for the rest of us?" a voice called out.

Aikur turned to look up at the top of the hill where he had just come from and saw Paavo standing and staring at the ruined camp site. The scout bent over, his chest heaving for breath. Krip appeared a few seconds later, his face flushed red and dripping with sweat.

"Good heavens," Krip shouted. "Hold up Aikur, you don't need to win the fight in one night."

Aikur snarled and turned to sit on the log.

The others trudged down the hill toward him and plopped down on the log on either side of the large warrior.

"I suppose you weren't boasting when you told those recruits you could have taken the lot of them," Krip commented coolly. The man pulled out a flask of water and drained a good amount before wiping the sweat from his brow, incidentally combing his matted hair off to one side. "I'm sorry it had to come to this," Krip said, holding the flask out for Aikur.

Aikur shook his head. He didn't want a drink, he wanted all of the goblins dead. Nothing else would sate him now.

"There is another camp about ten miles farther into the mountains," Paavo said. "Or at least there used to be. It's the only real settlement I know of that the goblins keep semi-permanently. Every other clan in these mountains moves around continuously. One of my comrades spoke of an ogre out this way somewhere, but I haven't seen any sign of such a beast."

Aikur nodded. "Ten miles... we can make that by nightfall. When they sleep, we strike."

"Tonight?" Krip asked. "Some of us aren't as young as we used to be."

"Then stay here and wait for Captain Marsten," Aikur said flatly.

Krip arched a brow. "No, I think I would rather go with you, my friend."

Aikur didn't respond. He sat for a few moments longer, calculating his timing for the next ten miles. If everything went well, they would only have to wait long enough to survey the next site before attacking. Encouraged by the prospect of clearing an entire clan, Aikur rose from the log and began walking.

"Wait for me," Paavo said. "I'll have to find the trail and lead you there."

Krip grunted while standing, but otherwise voiced no complaints as he put away his water flask and hurried to catch up with the others.

They walked through the forest for several hours, carefully picking their way through trees and then following alongside a cool, clear mountain brook before veering off slightly to the east along a mountain ridge. Aikur spotted numerous mountain goats and a herd of elk as they crossed several game trails through large clearings and dense patches of raspberry bushes that had obviously been eaten into, with bare, gnarled stubs poking out of the dirt in a much wider circle than what now stood.

As the sun dropped down, the ridge wound around the middle of a tall mountain, leading them into a nook between two peaks that was heavily wooded with pines and aspens. Twilight's shadow fell quickly over the area, cooling the air and signaling to Aikur that they were close to their target. As they made their way deeper into the forest Aikur spied cliffs leading up to a bluff overlooking the forest valley. Soon they found a pair of large caves, Paavo stopped and turned to the caverns, pointing and giving hand signals.

"In there?" Krip asked.

Paavo frowned, obviously perturbed that Krip was speaking instead of using signals. The scout put a finger over his lips and then gestured back to the cave on the right.

Aikur pulled his axe. Had there been a camp in the forest, he would have surveyed the area and strategized the best approach. If these goblins were all holed up in a cave, then there was little he could do but go in after them through the front door. The large Konnon started toward the cave, but Paavo stuck out an arm and held up two fingers.

The scout then pulled his bow and aimed toward the cave.

Aikur looked back to the cave, but he couldn't see any goblins, so either Paavo had better vision than him, or he knew something Aikur didn't.

Paavo let the arrow fly and quickly reloaded. The arrow struck against the side of the cliff and bounced off with a faintly audible *klink!*

A large goblin carrying a crude, spiked club emerged from the cave and looked around.

Paavo sent his second arrow, striking the goblin sentry in the head and killing him. "Now we can move," Paavo whispered. "Keep your wits about you, it's going to be darker in there than we are used to out here."

Aikur led the way, surveying the area around and half-expecting more goblins to emerge from the tunnels, but none did. Aikur and the others moved into the cave slowly, trying to allow their eyes to adjust before delving in too quickly.

Inside there was a small table with a clay plate on top that was filled with what looked like bird bones, though it was difficult for Aikur to be certain since many of the bones had been broken and chewed through. The stool next to the table was of rudimentary design, but was fashioned out of bone instead of wood. The seat itself was fashioned out of an elk's pelvic bone. Beyond the furniture, a single torch hung from the wall just before the tunnel curved down and to the right.

Paavo kept his bow at the ready, walking just a step behind and to Aikur's right. Aikur led the way, his axe anxiously waiting to bite into any foe they might encounter. Around the corner, Aikur was pleased to see a line of torches that gave off just enough light he could be comfortable. It had been a long time since he had been in the volcanic forges of his home town, but he still felt comfortable enough in the darkness. The only real difference was instead of smelling the heat, metal, and ash, these tunnels reeked of musk and damp.

The tunnel descended deeper than Aikur would have guessed from the outside, sprawling out another two miles before they came to a side chamber connected to the main tunnel by a short, twenty-yard cave. Aikur crept to the corner and looked around, spying two goblins sitting at a table and squabbling over what appeared to be a hunk of venison. After a moment, the far goblin punched the other right in the nose, knocking the wretched creature onto the ground. The victorious goblin then jumped up and shouted something in his unintelligible language before taking a grand bite of the raw flesh.

"Two goblins, one standing, one lying down," Aikur told Paavo.

Paavo nodded and put one arrow between his teeth while he set another. He stepped out around the corner and fired the first. A split-second later he fired the second arrow. Aikur smiled as the first arrow caught the standing goblin in the throat and the second zipped downward to take down the other goblin before it had even registered what had happened.

"Onward?" Paavo asked.

Aikur nodded. They walked down another fifty yards before the tunnel veered off sharply to the right and opened up into an impossibly large chamber.

"By the gods," Krip murmured as they stepped out onto a precipice overlooking a thousand foot drop into nothingness.

Before them a bridge of bone, wood, and rope stretched out to a large stalactite hanging from the ceiling. Walkways had been constructed into the stalactite, with several cave-like openings carved into it as well. From there, another bridge spanned the remaining gap to reach a kind of plateau that rose from the chasm below like a great table-top mountain. The edge was fenced in with wood and bone pikes, and inside the fence was a city of huts made from what appeared to be leather and other bits of cloth. Aikur could see numerous goblins walking around on the island of stone, going about their business as usual, entirely oblivious to the intruders.

"We could cut the rope bridge and strand them," Krip suggested.

"No," Aikur said quickly. "They built the bridge once, they can do it again. We have to get to them and destroy them."

"They might see us crossing the bridge," Krip said.

Aikur nodded. "It's about a hundred yards to the stalactite, and another hundred from there to the settlement."

"Nightfall won't help us," Paavo said. "They probably burn their torches and fires all the time."

"Well, you two can stay if you like," Aikur said. "I'm going to go knock on the door."

"What door?" Krip asked.

Aikur stepped out onto the bridge, axe in hand and ready for action. The planks held strong, but the bridge swayed under his shifting weight, swinging gently from side to side as he crossed. Paavo had of course followed him immediately, but Krip had hesitated a few seconds. Not that it bothered Aikur; he hadn't asked them to come along in the first place. This was *his* war. Lord Consuert and everyone else would have to wait their turn.

The large Konnon made it across the bridge without raising any alarms. He ascended the wood and bone planks around the stalactite and peered into the various dens he had seen from afar to find they were nothing more than storage rooms. Barrels, chests, and boxes of all shapes and sizes filled each den. He could only guess what was inside, but he was certain the goblins hadn't made the containers themselves. It looked more like stolen loot accumulated over decades of marauding and thieving in the mountains. When he made it to the second bridge, he noticed that there were two goblins talking on the opposite side. They were facing each other, with their sides to Aikur, but they were obviously guards of some sort as they both held spears and wore leather chest pads and helmets.

"Can you take those two?" Aikur asked.

"It's an easy enough shot since there is no wind to account for," Paavo said. "You want me to do it now, or wait until we are closer? Someone might see their bodies before we reach the other side."

Aikur nodded. "I'm counting on it."

"You're mad," Krip said. "They'll cut the bridge out from under you."

"Perhaps," Aikur said. "You two should stay here. Cover me with your arrows for as long as you can, and Krip, make sure no one comes in behind us."

"I hope you know what you're doing," Krip said.

"Good hunting," Paavo put in.

Aikur nodded and moved out onto the bridge. He had only taken a few steps when he heard one, then two faint whistling sounds overhead. Two seconds later the missiles fell on their targets. One of the goblin guards collapsed where he stood, but the other managed to stumble out through the narrow gap between the fence and the bridge. He toppled over and fell downward, still as a statue, disappearing into the darkness below.

The large Konnon started to jog across the bridge. The planks creaked and squeaked beneath him with each step he took as the bridge swayed and bounced.

A goblin emerged from a hut near the bridge with what appeared to be two half-dressed females clinging to his arms. The goblin stopped and stared at the guard's corpse, and then looked across the bridge to see Aikur.

"Kohn sikamar!" the goblin shouted. The two females dove back into the tent while the male pulled a sword and moved toward the bridge. "Kohn sikamar!" he shouted again.

A faint whistle split the air, and before the goblin could reach the guard's body, an arrow struck his heart and dropped him to the ground. A few goblins from within the settlement saw the commotion and took up the warning cry.

Shouts of "Kohn sikamar!" cut the silence and echoed off the caverns walls.

The two female goblins burst from their hut armed with spears and dressed in armor.

Aikur grinned as he ran faster for the other side. He had hoped the women-folk were warriors, for then he could repay in full the goblins that had murdered his wife.

The females sprinted nimbly onto the bridge, closing the distance much faster than Aikur was, but he didn't mind. He was saving his strength. So long as the goblins didn't cut the bridge down, it was a natural bottleneck that would give him an advantage over their larger numbers. Given the fact that they had so many full storage rooms on the other side of this bridge, he hoped they would only cut it down as a last resort. Then again, if they did cut it, there were worse things than death.

The first female closed in, her eyes red with anger and the veins in her neck and forehead bulging out of her grotesque, green skin. She stabbed at Aikur, but the move was clumsy. He parried with the top of his axe and then countered by slamming the pommel of his battle axe into the goblin's jaw. So forceful was his blow that the goblin flew up and over the edge of the bridge, screaming as she fell to her death.

The second goblin pulled a crude crossbow from behind her and fired, but Aikur managed to step to the side of the bridge and let the bolt sail by harmlessly. He then jumped up and down, causing the bridge to heave like an ocean's wave, knocking the goblin off balance when she tried to step forward. The creature stumbled and fell to her face, exposing her neck and back, which Aikur exploited quickly, driving his axe into the back of her skull and neck.

By this time, Paavo had fired several more arrows. Aikur looked up to see three goblins lying on the bridge, and several more back on the plateau.

"I'm out," Paavo shouted after a while. "Shall I join you?"

Aikur looked back to see Paavo drawing his short swords, but Aikur shook his head. "Stay there, guard the rear. This fight is mine!"

When he turned back to the goblins, he noticed that four of them had loaded bows and were arching back to compensate for distance. A second later they fired. Aikur, knowing he couldn't outrun the arrows or move nearly enough to the side to get out of their path, picked up the female goblin's body and hoisted her up like a shield as he knelt down beneath her corpse. Several jolts of force pounded the body, but nothing reached him. Aikur watched as the goblins reloaded and fired two more volleys before deciding to use another tactic.

"Kosmekah!" one of the goblins shouted, hoisting a sword high in the air.

Aikur grinned and dropped the body. "That's right, come get a taste," he said, rising to his feet and taking up his axe in his right hand while grabbing the fallen goblin's spear with his left.

The goblins fought each other, pushing and shoving to get onto the bridge. The writhing mass rushed out to meet him, but could only stand two goblins wide along the bridge, as it was far too narrow to allow more. A couple goblins even managed to trip and fall before reaching the bridge, which only made Aikur laugh as he calmly walked toward the heaving line of gnashing yellow teeth and buggy, bulging eyes advancing toward him.

As the goblins came within twenty feet, Aikur launched the spear, catching the lead goblin in the shoulder. It wasn't a lethal injury, but it caused that goblin to stop, which then got him trampled as the others clambered over him to get at Aikur. Several of the gruesome creatures tripped and created a sizeable pile-up that slowed the rest of the group. Aikur smiled and then gripped his axe with two hands. He swept horizontally, gashing one goblin across the chest and cutting through a second goblin's neck. Both goblins fell, creating yet another pile-up that gave Aikur the advantage. He slammed one, then another, and then took several steps back, putting distance between him and the surging group, allowing them to fight against each other to reach him. Goblins were easy targets, but tired and clumsy goblins were even easier.

A spear flew through the air at Aikur, but the large man ducked and deflected with his axe. A moment later a short goblin lunged up to strike Aikur, but the large Konnon kicked the creature in the chest, sending him back to knock into four other goblins, taking them all down and creating another blockage.

Two more goblins squeezed through, but Aikur had plenty of time to react. He cleaved the first goblin's head in half, slicing off everything above the nostrils and sending the gore flying. Then, using his momentum he spun around and lashed out with a back spinning kick that caught the second goblin in the right shoulder and knocked him off the bridge. A few more burst through the blockage to get at him next, but Aikur cut the first with an overhead chop that buried his axe into the goblin enough that he could swing the entire corpse on the end of his weapon. He first turned left, slamming into a goblin and nearly knocking it from the bridge, and then he swung right, knocking two more down to the planks before the corpse came free of the blade and slipped off to fall on top of the others.

Aikur pulled his axe back, leveled it so that the point atop the blades was aimed like a spear, and then jabbed two more goblins in the throat and face. So quick and strong were his strikes that goblin bodies piled up in front of him like a fleshy green wall, but for every pile he made, ten more goblins pushed their way onto the bridge. He fought for several more minutes, hewing down foe after foe without taking a single hit himself, and then backing up a few steps to allow more of the buggars onto the bridge.

Then, just as he came within twenty yards of the stalactite, Aikur smiled. He could see that the last of the goblin warriors had made it onto the bridge, too enraged by his attack to see what he had led them to. Aikur quickly dispatched four more goblins and pushed their bodies back into the swelling crowd to buy himself two seconds of time. Then he spun around. He seized the guide rope at his left and came down hard on the rope at his right with his axe. The blade cut through the supports as easily as if it had been made of a single thread. The bridge jerked and spun, sending at least a dozen goblins flying over the side.

"Are you insane!?" Krip shouted.

Aikur wasn't listening. He had a plan, and it would work. He turned and cut the other guide rope and then held on with all of his strength as his body went weightless for half a second. Then the bridge fell out from beneath him for a moment before he too began to fall.

Goblins shrieked and screamed all around him as they fell to their deaths.

Aikur clung to the rope and somehow managed to hitch his battle axe to the harness on his back so he could use both hands. The bridge accelerated as it swung through the darkness, but the large Konnon kept his grip. As they careened toward the cliffside he realized that he would need something to absorb the shock, and he only had a couple of seconds to figure it out. He maneuvered to grip a plank a couple feet up and then began climbing the planks as if they were rungs on a ladder. He encountered a goblin a few feet up, but the creature didn't notice him for it had its eyes closed and was clinging to the rope with both hands and its legs. Aikur reached up and socked the goblin in the groin from below, which made the thing release its grip and fall. Aikur then continued climbing.

The next goblin pulled a dagger and clumsily swung at Aikur to keep him at bay, but Aikur grabbed the goblin by his ankle and yanked hard. The first tug produced no results, but the second ripped the goblin from the bridge entirely. Aikur snarled at the next goblin up, who had just watched the other be pulled from the bridge, but instead of fighting back the goblin only squeaked and scaled around the bridge to hang onto the underside by the planks, hoping to avoid its comrade's fate. Aikur smiled.

Perfect.

Aikur climbed up and quickly grabbed onto the goblin's hands from his side of the bridge. At first the goblin's eyes went wide, as if it expected a killing blow any second, but then it knit its brow at Aikur for a moment before turning around.

It let out a feral scream that could have woken the dead as they swung the last few yards toward the cliff side. Aikur braced himself for impact, aligning his body with the goblin's to absorb as much of the crash as possible.

There was a sickening cascade of crunching bones and rupturing tissues that cut the goblin's blood-curdling scream short. Though it helped to have the goblin in front of him, Aikur still felt the wind pushed from his lungs upon impact. He nearly let go, slipping two rungs downward before he could force himself to focus just enough to cling to a thick plank.

Other goblins screamed above him. Some of them fell off, others had been crushed on the wrong side, and a few lucky ones managed to stay on the bridge. After a few moments of struggling for breath, his lungs inflated once more and energy flooded through him. He rested his forehead against the plank and coughed a couple times before daring to look up.

There was a goblin about ten feet above him that was dangling upside-down with its ankle caught in the ropes and another couple of scattered goblins farther up the bridge. None of them looked too sure of themselves at the moment, and better yet they didn't even seem to register that Aikur was still on the bridge with them.

He took in a deep breath and looked up to the top. He was still a good seventy yards from the top, but he could make that as long as no one cut the bridge above him. Hand over hand he climbed up the planks, working his toes into the spaces between the rough-cut wood as best he could for footholds. After a few seconds, the dangling goblin noticed him and just stared wide-eyed. Aikur winked at the creature and then punched the goblin in the face, shattering the wretched thing's nose and knocking it unconscious. He continued up the bridge, following after a couple of goblins that had finally started the ascent themselves.

After a while, one of them looked down and saw Aikur gaining on them.

"Hosaka menaw!" the goblin shouted.

Aikur redoubled his climbing efforts, but it was no use. Three goblins part way up the bridge were now working furiously to cut the ropes with daggers and dislodge the portion below them, sawing back and forth as fast as their skinny green arms could move to keep Aikur from reaching them. The large Konnon made it to the goblin that had sounded the alarm and reached for the thing's leg, but it pulled its feet up and then kicked at Aikur. The goblin was fairly weak to begin with, but given the angle of attack, the creature was entirely ineffective. Aikur took a couple soft hits on the shoulder and the top of his head and then timed his move so that he would reach up and grab the goblin after a kick. Aikur seized the thing around the ankle and yanked hard enough that the goblin's knee popped out of joint and the thing let go of its hand holds. Aikur tossed the flailing goblin out into the abyss and then continued upward.

The guide rope on the right snapped.

The bridge swung out to the left, hanging Aikur precariously over the chasm. He looked up and realized there was no way he could reach the next goblin in time. The rope on the left side was fraying badly and some of the fibers were beginning to explode apart before being cut due to the weight they now supported.

Aikur looked to the stone wall in front of him and made a split-second decision. Rather than fall, he was going up the cliff. He scrambled around the back of the bridge and then reached out for a stone lip. Just as the fingers of his left hand gripped the lip, the other side of the bridge came loose. Aikur let go and held to the rock as a few of the planks struck his back and then fell beyond him.

The goblins, pleased with their plan and believing that Aikur had fallen to his doom, shouted and cheered, and then began climbing upward once more along the bridge.

Aikur held still, hoping that perhaps they couldn't see him. Then, after a few seconds he looked up to check on his enemies. The last one was just clambering over the top. Aikur dragged himself up along the cliff face, using small ledges and angled cracks to hold onto. His forearms burned after only a few feet, but he had expected that. He was a large man, and was not accustomed to using his muscles this way. Still, he focused on the goblins that had gotten away.

"Three warriors," Aikur said. "Three more to kill." He pulled himself upward until at last he reached the remaining portion of the bridge. He reached out and grabbed onto it. Instantly his forearms felt better as he now had much larger supports to hold onto. His ascent quickened, and he reached the top in just a couple more minutes of climbing. All the while he was listening for any hint of his enemies. Hearing nothing, he decided to risk coming right over the top and onto the plateau. After all, he couldn't dangle over the chasm forever. Up and over he went, rolling across the solid plateau and sighing in relief upon seeing only the dead goblins that Paavo had slain with arrows waiting for him at the top.

He pushed himself up to his feet with a grunt and then trudged off toward the center of the settlement. The huts and small towers around him were so crude and basic that it perplexed him any of these creatures could have bested his wife. Had they surrounded her? Poisoned her somehow? Or perhaps she had the morning sickness from being pregnant and couldn't fight to the best of her abilities.

A sound from a hut on the right caught his attention. It wasn't loud, but it was distinct, like a whimper or a cry. He pulled his axe from the harness and used it to hook the cloth flap covering the entryway and pull it back. Inside he saw a disheveled, wrinkled goblin with thinning gray hair and dim eyes sitting in front of two small goblin infants. The old goblin stretched out its arms as if to shield the infants with its own body.

Aikur took two steps closer to inspect the rest of the hut. There were no beds to speak of, at least not proper ones. There was only an old quilt along the ground with a few dirty blankets folded at the end. There was a small wooden box to the left, filled with large wooden balls, a club, and what looked like a doll with hair made of straw. Seeing the doll made Aikur recall Dezri's stuffed animal. He looked back to the old goblin, who still sat defiantly, protecting the younglings.

"No," Aikur said with a shake of his head. "I'm not like you. Not even now." He backed away and let the flap fall closed. No matter how deep his hatred, he couldn't kill the defenseless infants. It wasn't right. He walked beyond several rows of huts until he found the three escaped goblins standing behind one of the huts and seemingly arguing amongst themselves. One of them thumped its chest and then slapped another goblin in the face, but that didn't seem to settle it. Instead, the two drew knives while the third took a step back and watched.

Aikur let the knife fight play out as the two competitors hacked and slashed at each other for the better part of two minutes, each scoring a hit on the other every once in a while across the forearm or shoulder. Then, they rushed each other and became so entangled as they hit the ground that it was impossible for Aikur to know who was winning. After a few moments, the goblin on top went stiff and its eyes shot open wide. It moaned and then fell to the side. The other goblin jumped up and shouted as it pumped its hands into the air.

It then saw Aikur and the victorious snarl faded from its face, replaced by an open-mouthed stare. Aikur rushed in.

The goblins, to their credit, didn't run away. They charged with only their daggers.

They should have run.

Aikur killed them both in a matter of seconds. He then spun around in place, looking at the other huts nearby. How many more of them were here? In no particular order, Aikur began tearing down the front flaps on each hut. Many of the living spaces were empty, some had only infants, and others had elderly goblins. Occasionally they had both an elderly goblin and an infant or two inside. Whenever he found an adult, he made it move into the center of the settlement, carrying the infants with it.

He wasn't going to hurt the infants, but he didn't want to end up being surrounded by angry goblins either. It was better to maintain situational control than to let a false sense of security enable an age-stricken goblin to fire a crossbow at him.

After about an hour, he came to the largest hut in the settlement. Wailing and crying went up from some of the elders gathered in the center of the settlement, but none of them made a move to stop him. Aikur walked up and noticed that this particular hut had wooden doors. As he examined it closer, he discovered that it not only had doors, but the hut wasn't built with leather and cloth walls. Underneath the patchwork flaps were walls made of wood as well.

"The chief's hut," Aikur muttered to himself. He moved to the front door and kicked it in. A pair of young, adult goblin females yelped and jumped back to protect a group of goblin younglings. These were not infants, but children. Aikur stepped inside and looked at the terrified youngsters staring at him. He then looked to the women, who were scantily clad in clothes made from animal fur that barely covered the essentials. They were not fighters as the others had been. They had no weapons, and they looked as frightened as the children.

Aikur took in a breath and surveyed the group. Thirty children in all. That number added to the seventeen infants outside, along with the eight old goblins and the two adult females in here and there was quite a large number of survivors. Survivors that would never forget his face. They would grow up, and one by one, or perhaps en masse, they would come looking for him, just the way he had come looking for their parents.

Suddenly he found his rage dissipating.

He saw a young goblin, no bigger than Dezri, reach out and cling to one of the females. It formed a tiny little green fist as it half-buried its face in the woman's leg. It was the fist that struck Aikur the hardest. In an instant, he saw not the goblin, but his own son. A tiny little fist the same shape as Dezri's, and a pair of green eyes looking up to him now.

Aikur held up his left hand, and then slowly put away his axe with the other. "It's over," he said.

One of the young goblin women relaxed a bit, and then pointed to a box near the front of the building.

"Ekat lodun," she said.

Aikur shook his head. "Don't understand you," he said.

She moved forward and Aikur reflexively gripped his axe handle with his right hand. The female paused and held up her hands, gesturing to the box with her chin.

"Ekat lodun," she said again.

Aikur let her move to the box. She reached down with one hand and pried the lid open to reveal hunks of gold and silver.

"Ekat lodun," she repeated again as she pulled out a hunk of gold and then held it out to Aikur.

He looked at the precious ore and then shook his head. "No, I don't want your things," he said. "I only wanted..." he caught himself and stopped talking. What would he say? He only wanted to destroy them all because they might have had something to do with his wife's murder? They wouldn't understand his words anyway. He walked backward to the door and then ducked out from the hut. As he spun around, he saw the eight elderly goblins kneeling in front of the hut, each holding necklaces or rings made of gold as if offering him payment. "I'm not here for your gold," he said. Aikur walked back to the destroyed bridge and looked out over the chasm.

Paavo and Krip were gone.

Chapter 8

Aikur stood staring across the chasm for some time, not sure how he was going to get back across. Then again, he hadn't necessarily expected to live through the encounter. If this was the group that had destroyed Jeriston, then the war was over. Revenge for his family and Jeriston had been served, and it had been easy. He frowned. It had been ridiculously easy, now that he thought about it. Sure, he was a Konnon, born and bred for war, but the goblins had been easier to defeat than even he had predicted.

What's more, the fear he saw in their eyes did not show a savage race.

What had Lord Consuert been so worried about? Were there more warriors out roaming the countryside? It was certainly possible that a proper army was out pillaging while the town defenders remained behind, but even then, it was too simple.

The large Konnon stopped then and turned around. The eight elders were watching him, but had not moved from their position outside the wooden hut. The female that had offered him the gold had come out and was directing the other to gather the infants as well.

Gold. Why had she offered gold?

Aikur grit his teeth as a wild idea came into his head.

The large Konnon walked back toward the elders, keeping his hands visibly away from his axe and doing his best not to look imposing, which was difficult when his shoulders were nearly half as wide as some of the elders were tall. As he approached they each knelt back down and again offered their jewelry. Aikur pointed to the female and motioned for her to come to him. She stood, staring at him with her black eyes and frowning, obviously contemplating refusing.

Aikur stepped close to one of the elderly females and reached down to her bony, green fingers. He closed the goblin's hand around the jewelry and then pushed it back toward the goblin.

"I don't want that," he said.

The other elders looked confused.

One of them spoke to the others, but another quickly shushed him.

The young female goblin moved toward Aikur. He pointed back to the chasm and mimed the bridge falling with his hands. "How do I get out of here?"

The female cocked her head to the side.

Aikur grunted. "Come with me," he said, waving for her to follow him. He took two steps and then looked back to see she was still standing where she had been. He looked down to the dirt at their feet and a new idea came to him. "Very well." He went back toward the female and then bent down to draw with his finger in the dirt. "This is where we are," he said as he drew a crude looking plateau. He then moved his hand left and drew a stalactite. "This is where I came from," he said as he moved to draw the precipice and the long cave he had used to enter the goblin's territory. He drew the bridges and then a stick figure to represent himself. "This is me. I want to go back here, but the bridge is gone." Aikur mimed everything with his hand and then wiped away the first bridge. "How do I get out?" Aikur asked.

The elders looked to each other, a couple of them mumbling something indistinguishable under their breaths. The young female looked at the picture in the dirt for a moment, and then grunted and waved her arm for Aikur to follow.

"Emok ereh," she said.

One of the elders waved a hand and barked something at the young female goblin, but she snarled at him. Aikur watched the older goblin bow its head. None of the others spoke.

"Emok ereh," the female said again.

Aikur followed her back into the wooden building. The younglings looked up at Aikur with the same fear they had before, but they were not huddled together this time. Now they were spread out along the walls, sitting down as if waiting for something to do. The contrast between the goblins and his own people was striking. Here, the elderly and the young didn't fight. They were entirely putting their fate in Aikur's hands. On New Konnland, had a band of Kottri managed to slay all of the warriors outside and storm into a city, even the five year olds would have fought to defend themselves. It was impossible to fathom how the goblins could let one single warrior conquer everything. If they didn't have a larger army outside somewhere, then they were not shaping up to be half as savage as Aikur had expected.

"Emok ereh," the female said once more as she moved to the back of the building and pulled back a set of black bear furs to reveal a short door. Aikur narrowed his eyes at the portal, for it wasn't set into the rear wall. It was several feet in from that, and looked as though it led to a cellar of some sort. The female goblin grabbed a torch from the wall nearby and opened the doors.

A gust of dry, warm air flowed out from the doors and brushed over Aikur.

"Sihtyaw," the female said before stepping into the doorway and going down a steep set of stairs.

Aikur followed after her, grabbing a torch of his own for good measure. He was not going to trust the goblin as his only source of light. He had to duck to avoid hitting his head on the ceiling and turn to the side to make his large feet fit upon the short, steep steps. The two of them descended twenty feet and came to a landing in a seven foot wide tunnel that wound like a corkscrew through the rock, going down deep. Neither of them spoke for the space of thirty minutes as they followed the path around and around. The air grew warmer, and stale, giving off a slight hint of sulfur as they reached the bottom where the tunnel sprawled out in a straight line.

"Where does this go?" Aikur asked.

The female goblin motioned for him to follow. "Dnal nus, emok, emok."

Aikur shook his head and followed after her, figuring he had come too far now not to see it through. After another ten minutes, a chamber opened up on the right. Aikur looked in and saw four goblin males sitting around a very large geode that had been broken to reveal the crystals inside. The turned and looked back at him, but they didn't jump or reach for weapons. In fact, they didn't have any weapons.

"Kosar do mah," the female said to them.

One of the males put a hand to his mouth, the other three hung their heads. Aikur then realized that the female must have told them of the destruction above, but if she had, then why weren't they angry? Why weren't they charging toward him?

The female continued on, beckoning for Aikur to follow. The four goblin males turned back to their massive geode and prostrated themselves before it, apparently calling out in some sort of prayer. Aikur followed after his guide and they continued walking through the tunnel. They passed another six chambers, each like the first with some sort of crystal or small pile of precious ore in the center and a group of goblins that appeared to be busy praying. Each time the reactions were the same. Some of the goblins would be stunned, and others would weep and hang their heads. After a few seconds, each group of goblins would turn back to praying, but none of them made a move against Aikur.

It occurred to the Konnon that perhaps this tunnel led to a dead end, and the plan was to lure him to a trap, but he never saw any weapons near any of these goblins, so unless they were going to fight him with only their hands, there wasn't much to be worried about.

After another half hour of walking, they did in fact come to a dead end.

Aikur reached around for his axe, but the goblin female strode up to the wall and hung her torch in a crude loop of iron attached to the side wall and then moved three paces to her right and slid aside a small covering in the wall to reveal a strange metal lever. She gripped it with both hands and leaned with her body, pulling the lever to the left. There was a series of clicks and pops as she pulled it into place. She then moved to the right wall and uncovered a second lever hidden in the wall. This one she pulled to the right. Along with the pops and clicks there was a puff of dust and dirt that fell from the ceiling on the far wall. Then, ever so slowly, a large circle of stone set into the wall began to roll to the side, revealing a short cave of maybe thirty yards that opened up to the forest outside.

"Do sinar ans truner reven erom," the female said. She pointed to the cave with one hand and then bowed her head.

Aikur looked at her, and then glanced back up the tunnel. Something in his gut told him that this was all very wrong. "Come here," Aikur said. He bent down to the dirt floor, setting his torch off to the side, and began drawing once more. Off to one side he drew a large mountain with a cave opening in it. To the left a few feet he drew the outline of a house, and then another stick figure to represent himself. "This is me, this is my home," he said. "This is your home," he said pointing to the female and then to the mountain he drew. He drew a shorter stick figure to represent the goblin. "This is you," he said. He then drew two more stick figures next to him, one for Karyna, and another for Dezri. "This is my wife and son." He paused, staring at the images in the ground for a moment before continuing. "Your people," Aikur said as he drew more goblins in the dirt. He made sure to give them spears to show they were warriors. "They came to my home and attacked." He dotted the dirt between the mountain and the house to show travel. Then he wiped the house, his wife, and Dezri away. "They killed my family. So I came here." Aikur circled the stick figure representing himself and then dotted the ground to show he followed the others. Then he wiped the goblin warriors from the dirt.

The female stood and stared at the drawing, rubbing her shoulders with her green hands as if suddenly cold. "Kosdarin, moktar," she said, shaking her head. She knelt down and redrew the mountain, this time putting the goblin warriors inside the outline of the mountain. She redrew Aikur's house and family as the large man stepped back to give her room. Next she drew a group of men on what appeared to be horses. She circled them and then pointed to her mountain. She made dots in the dirt from the horsemen to outside the mountain, and then drew dots from the goblin warriors to the same spot and drew an X. "Ereht rakams finigit ans werger." She then drew dots back into the mountain. Lastly she wiped away the dots that Aikur had used to represent goblins coming to his house and instead drew a long line and put her hands up like an X across her body. "Werm nigin der smeck. Werm nigin der smeck."

Aikur narrowed his eyes on her. He knew it was just as possible that she was lying, but if she was telling the truth, then it was apparent that she was saying her people had nothing to do with his family.

"No," Aikur said with a shake of his head. "No, you're trying to trick me." He got up and went for the exit without looking back. His anger was rising again. How dare the female try to claim innocence. Aikur had found goblin bodies at his home. His wife had followed them into the forest. He had seen all the proof he needed.

He could hear the stone sliding and scraping its way back into place, sealing off the passageway to the goblins' inner city once more as he continued through the short cave and stepped out into the forest. Night had settled upon the trees now, bringing with it a chill in the air, but Aikur didn't mind. He had spent many nights out in the elements before. He glanced back to the small cave and wondered why there was no goblin sentry posted here as there had been at the other entrance. Perhaps they believed the massive slab of stone was sufficient to keep intruders out.

Aikur turned toward the west and began walking. If he could, he needed to find Paavo and Krip to let them know everything he had done and seen. He walked for only a mile or so before he heard something in the bushes ahead of him. Aikur started to reach for his axe, but then stopped when he heard Krip's voice.

"We should find a place to spend the night," Krip said. "We'll be no good to anyone if we exhaust ourselves."

Aikur smiled. "Over here," he said loudly.

Paavo came around a tree and into view, grinning ear to ear as Krip came around the other side.

"Aikur!" Krip shouted as he rushed up to greet the man. "I wasn't sure we'd see you again."

"That was an incredible stunt you pulled with the bridge," Paavo commented. "How did you get out, did you find another bridge somewhere?"

Aikur shook his head. "No, they have a tunnel. It goes down through the plateau and then out the side of the mountain. It was a long trek, but uneventful."

"Really?" Paavo asked, his eyes glancing beyond Aikur and into the darkness. "Where does it come out, exactly?"

Aikur thumbed over his shoulder. "I can show you in the morning, but first we should set up camp. Do either of you have anything to eat?"

Krip pulled his bag around and started rummaging through it. "I have some food."

Paavo grabbed his water skin and tossed it to Aikur. "You must be thirsty, take what you need. There is a fast-running stream not far from here. I can refill it after you're done."

Aikur caught it and nodded his thanks as he uncapped the water skin and began to drink deeply of the cool water inside. He let the liquid rush through his throat until he had drained half of the container, then he wiped his mouth and tossed it back to Paavo. "Thanks," he said."

An owl hooted off in the trees nearby.

"This other entrance," Paavo began again. "Is it far from here?"

Aikur shook his head. "Maybe a mile, or just a bit farther," he replied. "The thing about the cave though is that it doesn't look like an entrance, it's sealed off with a secret door of sorts at the end of it."

"How did you get through then?" Paavo pressed.

"A goblin led me out," Aikur replied.

"A goblin?" Krip snorted. The veteran frowned and pulled out a piece of bread. "I wouldn't have thought you would have left any alive."

Aikur shrugged. "I killed every warrior they had," he said.

"So then this goblin that let you out, you killed him too?" Paavo asked.

Aikur shook his head. "It was a female, actually, and no. There are a handful of goblins left inside, but none that pose a threat."

Paavo grunted. "Then tomorrow we will go back in through this secret passage and finish the job," he said.

Aikur took the bread that Krip offered and then turned a hard stare on Paavo. "We'll let them be," he said. "The children are too small to cause any trouble," he said. "The elderly are far too old. There won't be any trouble from this lot again." He chose not to tell them of the female's denial that the goblins had ever attack in the first place. He still wasn't sure he believed her, though he had softened a bit toward the idea since leaving the cave and allowing himself time to cool off.

"No, Lord Consuert was clear. We have to wipe them out or drive them out. If they want to live, then they will need to go across the mountains and into the deserts in the east. We have no other choice."

Aikur took a bite of the dry bread and chewed it while thinking how to respond. He knew people in Kelsendale were different, but what possible reason could there be for wiping out the children? There was no honor in such atrocities.

"Did you see any gold?" Paavo asked.

Aikur stopped chewing. He glanced to Krip and saw the veteran had a confused look on his face, and then back to Paavo, who only pressed for an answer.

"Well?" Paavo insisted.

"What difference does that make?" Krip asked.

Aikur swallowed the half-chewed bite. "I saw some, but not much," he replied.

Paavo sighed and folded his arms. "What about in the secret tunnel. Did you see any sign of ore deposits, or mining perhaps?"

Aikur cocked his head to the side. "Why the sudden interest in gold?" the Konnon asked. "I thought the goal was to make our borders safe, or was there something you forgot to mention to Wallace?"

Krip tossed his sack on the ground. "Paavo, what is the meaning of this?"

Paavo shrugged. "If the mountain has wealth to offer, then Lord Consuert will want to know. It will help pay the wages for everyone who fought."

"You mean for everyone that is fighting," Aikur corrected. "This wasn't the group that sacked Jeriston. They were entirely unorganized. They wouldn't have been able to defeat an entire town, certainly not in one night either. So there must be another group out there somewhere," Aikur commented.

Paavo wagged a finger. "It has been a pleasure to work beside you, Konnon," Paavo said. "It's only too bad that your grief has driven you mad."

"Mad? What are you talking about, Paavo?" Krip put in.

Paavo shrugged. "It seems that when I arrived here, I was too late. Aikur was in a blind rage, and he turned on us. We had to defend ourselves, of course," Paavo said.

The hairs on the back of Aikur's neck stood on end.

An owl hooted in the distance once more.

Paavo lunged toward Krip and plunged his sword into the man's neck before Krip ever knew what was happening.

Aikur pulled his axe and started for Paavo, but a sharp pain struck his left leg. The large Konnon stumbled to the ground. Another biting pain stabbed at the left side of his back.

"Poor Aikur, driven mad by the loss of his family. He could have been a hero, but now he will be remembered only as a traitor," Paavo said as he turned toward Aikur, his sword glistening with Krip's blood.

Aikur looked to his friend. The crossbow bolts in his body must have been tipped with something, for his mind was beginning to blur and his senses were beginning to dull. The large warrior shook his head and put all the pieces together. "You staged the attack on my home," Aikur said.

"If it helps," Paavo said, "I'm sure your wife would have put up quite a fight had it been the goblins." Several men came into view from the trees around them, each with weapons drawn and ready to finish Aikur off. Aikur looked up at the man next to Paavo. His silhouette was familiar somehow, then it hit him.

"You were the one watching me in the church," Aikur said.

The man nodded.

"Pity you couldn't just follow orders," Paavo said. "A man of your talents would have done well under Lord Consuert. You could have had anything you wanted, and," Paavo paused for a moment, grinning eerily in the night. "I wouldn't have needed to kill your family."

The rage boiled up inside the Konnon once more. Now it all made sense. The goblins would never have defeated his wife. Karyna could have beaten two dozen of the things blindfolded, but treachery was not something a Konnon was accustomed to dealing with. In New Konnland, everyone fights for the same cause, and betrayal is entirely unheard of. The thought of stabbing an ally in the back would never even enter a Konnon's mind. Paavo had mentioned there were other scouts still in the area. It would have been easy to send them in for the attack. From there, with Paavo pretending to discover the murders at the same time, Aikur was too trusting, and it had been far too easy to direct him to this particular mountain. Aikur now knew the true motive as well. Gold.

"It all comes to greed," Aikur growled.

"There are only two reasons for war," Paavo replied. "You either need resources someone else has, or someone is trying to take yours without your permission. Everything else is just political propaganda."

"You denied my family final rites," Aikur said.

"Of course," Paavo replied. "I couldn't have you sulking about. I needed you angry. I needed your warrior spirit to soar higher than ever before, and it worked."

Aikur felt every muscle in his body tighten. "And Captain Marsten?" Aikur asked.

"Will give me a commendation for a job well done. We get the mountain, and we only lost three Konnons to do it…" Paavo stopped and looked at the others. "Well, and Jeriston."

Everyone laughed.

They laughed!

Aikur pushed up to his feet in an instant. His mind focused, honing in on his rage. He could hear his wife and son screaming again, but this time he knew who the enemy truly was. He jabbed out with the spike atop his battle axe, but Paavo leapt back just far enough to avoid being hit.

Twang!

Someone fired a crossbow bolt, but Aikur was not going to be stopped so easily now. He turned to the right and charged two of the scouts nearby. With one savage chop he cut through them both, sending their severed bodies to the ground in a heap. Heavy footsteps fell upon the ground behind him. He spun away just as a sword chopped downward through the air where he had been standing. Aikur hooked the back of the scout's leg with his axe and pulled, slicing partway through the ankle and dropping him to the ground. Aikur stomped the man's chest, cracking several ribs before stabbing the spike atop his axe through the scout's right eye socket.

Another scout charged in with a spear. Aikur let go of his axe, turned and wrapped his hands around the spear shaft and planting his feet. The shaft bent up in the middle as Aikur forced his enemy to stop, but just before the wood broke, Aikur whipped him to the side, throwing him to the ground. Aikur then flipped the spear over in his hands and masterfully launched it at another scout who was reloading a crossbow. The spear drove through the scout and nailed his corpse to a tree some two feet behind. Aikur ripped his axe free and then moved to the disarmed spearman, who was just pushing up to his feet. Aikur took the man's head in one swipe and then quick-stepped beyond the fallen scout to take down three more.

Paavo came in hard and fast from the right. Aikur turned to deflect, but not quickly enough. He caught a slice along the right shoulder after Paavo's sword glanced off the shaft of Aikur's axe. The pain ripped through Aikur, but rather than recoil, he lashed out with a front kick to Paavo's chest. Paavo staggered backward a couple feet, putting him in the right position for Aikur's next move. The large Konnon came down with a massive chop, catching Paavo in the chest and cutting down through the spine nearly to his pelvis before the blade got stuck in bone. Paavo fell to the ground without another sound, taking Aikur's axe with him.

Aikur took two steps forward, but then the effects of whatever poison the crossbow bolts had been tipped with caught up to him. His rapidly beating heart slowed. His vision blurred, and he fell to the ground. There was no way to know for certain how many days had passed, but the next time he opened his eyes, he was in a wooden cage, being carted off through town.

"Where am I?" Aikur asked.

A soldier smacked the side of the cage. "Shut up in there!"

Horse hooves clip-clopped their way up to the cage and a man leaned down from a tall, black horse. Aikur looked up at the man and guessed it was Captain Marsten.

"You made quite a mess of this operation," Captain Marsten said. "But don't worry, we'll finish breaking through that secret passageway and complete the remainder of the mission without you."

"Khefir take you," Aikur snarled.

Captain Marsten smiled. "Maybe he will and maybe he won't, but I think we both know that he most certainly will take *you*. After all, you betrayed your own countrymen. You killed Paavo and Krip, not to mention the other scouts sent to help you defeat the goblins. Why, not even Wallace will speak up for you now, traitor."

"So kill me and be done with it," Aikur said.

Captain Marsten shook his head. "No, that won't do. A traitor deserves a proper trial. You will, of course, be found guilty upon my own testimony. Then you will be executed for your crimes. Don't worry, the trial will only last a day or two before your sentencing, that I promise you. You will also be denied your final rites." Captain Marsten began laughing and trotting his horse away.

Chapter 9

As Captain Marsten had promised, the trial was efficiently short, and seemed little more than a formality designed as a show offered to the masses to distract them from Lord Consuert's true crimes. The room was packed with spectators, none of them from Aikur's town near the border, and the jury was made up of magistrates rather than peers, with an older judge presiding over them. Aikur had little doubt that each of them were bought and paid for from Lord Consuert's personal treasury.

"Does the condemned have any last words they wish for this court to hear?" the judge asked.

Aikur stood, his wrists chained and secured to an iron loop in the floor. He looked to the quorum of magistrates and then back to the judge. He shook his head disgustedly. "What should I say?" he began. "How can I explain to you the injustice that has been dealt to me? The fiendish designs of the gods and the brutish men who collaborated against me cannot easily be described in such a way as for you to understand the hell that is my life. I would wager that after my trial is complete, none of you will remember my name. You will not care that my wife and children were murdered by the same government officials I was duty-bound to fight for during their war against the cursed races that border our lands. To be used in such a manner is to make a mockery of a man's entire life. My life. I cannot hope that many will believe my words, either in this testimony, or in my arguments in the courts of Gilbrait. Death has finally found me, as it finds all who walk on this mortal plane. My hope is that perhaps someone will learn from my story, and your eyes will be opened."

"Take him away," the judge said decisively.

"I am not finished," Aikur said.

The judge leaned back in his chair and the guards exchanged glances with each other.

"You think that by sentencing me you have decided my fate. Tomorrow the crowds will gather in the main square outside of this courthouse. They will jeer at me, spit upon me, and chant for my death. The fat, filthy executioner will hide behind his hood of black as he raises the axe over my neck. Then the crowd will rise in a chorus of cheers when my head is severed from its place, and my life is extinguished." Aikur turned to look at the magistrates again. He shook his head and spit upon the floor. "I am void of any offense to the king, or to my fellow countrymen; that is, any offense that was unprovoked. The murder of my wife and child was not a crime that my spirit could allow to go unanswered. Even if you don't care about them, what of Jeriston? An entire town was destroyed for this false war! You should be clamoring for real justice, but you are too cowardly to take up the responsibility. *I* have slain those dastardly vermin responsible for their innocent blood, and for this you sentence me to die as a hated criminal."

"I have heard enough, take him away!" the judge ordered.

The guards moved forward, but Aikur stopped them with an icy glare. "I will go only when I am finished speaking. It is my right to speak and offer my final testimony."

"A final testimony is given for the condemned to confess and forsake their crimes!" the judge roared. "Not for some insane, delusional foreigner to spin a tall tale to cover his depravities."

115

Aikur stood tall. "I slew the men who murdered my family, yet you call it depravities! I have one more slight that I will yet give you all in answer for the crimes committed against me. I will not let Lord Consuert, or the unmerciful, ignorant peasants have the pleasure of watching me die."

"Take him away, now!" the judge hollered.

"I am done," Aikur told the guards as they roughly unhooked him from the floor and dragged him down to the dungeons below the courthouse.

"You think you can escape?" one of the guards said as they tossed him into his cell.

Aikur shrugged. "My quill please," he said.

The guards huffed and gave him an inkwell and sharpened quill. "You are going to use that to unlock the door, is that it?" the guard teased. "Go ahead and try it. I'd love to have any excuse to kill you myself, traitor." The guard spit on Aikur's left cheek.

Aikur sneered at him. The guards left promptly, laughing and joking about how fun it would be to slit a Konnon's throat. Aikur turned and pulled a leather-bound book from under the blanket he used as a bed. He had spent the last couple of nights writing down his account of what had actually happened. He spoke of his wife and child, and also confessed that he had wrongfully assumed the goblins were to blame, and their blood was upon his head. Over the next several hours, he wrote down the remainder of his final testimony and then sighed. He took the quill and looked at the point.

"I may not be able to escape alive," he said to himself. "But I can decide the manner of my death." He slowly moved the point of the quill to his neck. Suicide was not the way of a Konnon, for they believed that such cowardice would condemn their soul to Hammenfein, but then, his family was already trapped there, having been denied their final rights. Even if Nagé would be willing to take him to Volganor to find rest in the Heaven City, he could not bear the idea of eternal separation from his family. "No crowds will get the pleasure of seeing my head roll. I will meet a death of my own making."

Aikur sat in his cell, his back against the cold, stone wall. He let his head fall back and closed his eyes. His hands trembled as the rage still burned through his blood and quickened his pounding heart. The point of the quill pressed into the left side of his neck, jabbing ever so slightly into his vein. He took a breath to steady his nerves.

He stopped short when he heard the soft, padded steps of someone coming down the hall. He slipped the quill under his leg and closed his eyes so as not to draw attention to himself. He didn't want to risk a guard catching him and either preventing him, or stopping the bleeding. The steps stopped in front of his cell and something tapped against the bars.

"Do you wish to see a priest?" a low voice called from the hallway.

"What need do I have of a priest?" Aikur replied without opening his eyes to regard the visitor.

"You are a Konnon, are you not?" the man asked. "Do you not follow the ways of Icadion?"

Who was this? Captain Marsten had been clear that final rites would be denied him.

Aikur slowly opened his eyes and turned an icy stare toward the intruder. He saw a man standing in taupe robes, hood drawn over the face, hands barely poking out from the oversized sleeves, and a large amulet dangling from the man's neck. "I have no need of a priest," Aikur said harshly.

The man raised a finger in the air. "But, a Konnon who does not receive the last rites is unable to traverse the rainbow bridge, or enter into paradise. As you are a descendant of those tribes cursed to wander the world, you need the last rites in order to gain favor in Icadion's eyes."

117

"As did my wife and child, but no one offered to help them," Aikur growled. "I would rather wander the fiery halls of Hammenfein with my family than make the journey to Volganor alone with the knowledge that they can never follow."

"I was not involved with your family," the priest said. "If you tell me where they are, I can go and offer the rites for them as well."

Aikur jumped up to his feet and marched to take hold of the bars on the door. The priest reflexively backed away several paces. "Would you go to the front lines then?" Aikur asked. "Would you risk life and limb among the goblins and the traitorous soldiers that infest the mountains? For that is where you will have to go. Even then, you won't be able to find a grave. You will have to find every part of their dismembered bodies in order to do anything for them. It would be easier to retrieve their souls from hell, than to recover them from the battle field."

"You may be right," the priest said resolutely. Something in his tone quieted the fires in Aikur's heart and piqued the large Konnon's curiosity.

"Why do you torment me?" Aikur asked.

"Have you heard of King Mathias, the one they call Mathias the Just, and Mathias the Wise?" the priest asked. "He was an old king in Engleah."

"All children have heard of his tales," Aikur replied.

The priest folded his arms and stepped in closer. "I was intrigued by the tales as a boy, and I thought what an exemplar of wisdom he was. Imagine, a king who might disguise himself and go out among his people to better judge them and learn the truth of their complaints."

"That kind of justice exists only in fables," Aikur hissed.

"I was present in your trial," the priest continued. "Did you mean what you said in your final testimony?"

Aikur's knuckles whitened and his arm muscles tensed against the unyielding bars. "Every word I spoke is true. My family was murdered so Lord Consuert could gain another gold mine." He pushed away from the door. "How does that sit with your sense of justice?"

The priest slowly reached up and pulled his hood back, revealing his face. Aikur stood bewildered at first, his eyes transfixed on the priest's face. Then, he remembered his senses and he dropped his gaze to the floor. He had seen the man once before, when he and Karyna had first made landfall in Kelsendale. Except the last time Aikur had seen him, the man had not been wearing the robes of a priest, he had been wearing a crown, and was accompanied by an impressive entourage. "My king, why have you..." the question faded away unfinished as Aikur's voice quavered.

"I have tried to emulate the king for whom many of my predecessors were named. When I heard of your trial, how could I not come and see it for myself?" The king reached up and produced a key from his left pocket. "I have the power to pardon, and release you."

Aikur shook his head. "I am eternally grateful, but I cannot accept. A life without my family is already a hell. Better to perish in the morning, and join them."

The king nodded. "I have many privileges as king," he said. "Not the least of which is access to ancient records and texts, some of which have been collected from the most remarkable sources. As you are aware, I come from a long line of kings loyal to Icadion. As such, we have written texts directly from Icadion, his son Lysander, and many other incredible texts that are hundreds or even thousands of years old, and yet the wisdom in these writings has enabled me, and my ancestors before me, to help our people. Now, I can use one of these writing to help you, and right an incredible wrong perpetrated against you by a wicked man. I think this may be of interest to you." He pulled a small, folded parchment from his other pocket. It crinkled and crackled as the king unfolded the document. "There is a parchment which was written a long time ago, and kept in the archives in my palace. It told of a possible way to reach a back door to Hammenfein." He held it up to the light and his eyes scanned over the page.

"There is but one way to the planes of hell," Aikur countered.

The king ignored him and looked over the parchment he held. "This is a transcription of the original. It is short, and not incredibly detailed, but it does talk about a way to sneak into Hammenfein, and release souls that have been imprisoned there."

Aikur stepped forward. "Is this a cruel joke, that you tease me with such a possibility?"

The king shook his head. "I do not know if it is true, but I thought that a man like you would want to know of its existence. If, as you say, you are ready to spend eternity in Hammenfein after facing the executioner's block, then perhaps you should go in person and knock on Hatmul's door. Go and see if it is possible to get your family back." The king held out the parchment.

Aikur took it and looked over the contents. "I expected a longer text," he said.

The king nodded. "It is short, but it is direct. My scholars believe the original was written by Kyra after Trystan was imprisoned in Hammenfein."

"Kyra? You mean Icadion's daughter?" Aikur asked.

The king nodded and smiled. "She was betrothed to marry Trystan, another god of good and noble birth. However, Hatmul tricked Trystan into coming to Hammenfein, where he imprisoned him and prevented the two from marrying. Kyra planned to infiltrate Hammenfein and rescue her love, but Trystan was killed before she could act on her plans. However, if anyone would know the way to sneak in, it would be her."

Aikur nodded. "If this is true, why did you not pardon me publicly in the court? Why wait until after my sentencing?"

"If this is true, I could not risk other, less savory men discovering the parchment's existence. Imagine the kind of frenzy that would incite." The king shook his head. "No, that would not have been wise. Now, I can release you in secret. Officially, you are being passed directly into my custody, but in reality you are free to pursue this if you wish." The king pointed to the parchment.

Aikur nodded. "What do you want of me?"

"I expect you to get them back. Bring their spirits out to the world of the living."

"But I will be unable to rejoin their spirits with their bodies."

The king nodded. "I will have a pair of priests waiting for you at Belknap. Get your family there and then my priests will call upon Nagé to open the bridge for you and your family to cross into Volganor." The king then held up a finger. "But be warned, Nagé will only do this once, as she promised me a favor for something I did for her long ago. Use this gift wisely, for it is not often that we can open the bridge."

Aikur folded the parchment and tucked it into his trousers. "Are you sure they can get us into Volganor? We won't be safe if we just go to the plane of the dead. Hatmul would be able to reach us there."

The king smiled wide. "If you can get through Hatmul's guards and hell hounds, my priests can get you across the rainbow bridge. On occasion, the gods have unlocked the bridge for kings or other great men to pass a few at a time." The king inserted the key and twisted it. The lock popped open and the door creaked outward.

"Understand, I can send a troop with you as far as Mat'Jhar, but from that point onward, you will be on your own. As brave as my men are, I cannot expect them to risk their souls by trespassing in Hatmul's domain."

"I understand," Aikur said. "And what of Lord Consuert?"

"Lord Consuert has already been stripped of his title and rank. His manor and lands are forfeit, and he will come back to Graebner where he will face a public trial, most likely followed by execution, or perhaps banishment to the nesting grounds."

A tear fell from Aikur's cheek. "I have no words to thank you appropriately."

The king slapped a hand to Aikur's shoulder. "See to your family, and that will be thanks enough for me."

"I will do better than that," Aikur said. "I will tell the hosts of Volganor what you are doing for me, and your name will be exalted in the highest halls of heaven."

"Come," the king said. "Let me show you out of this prison and to the armory. I have reclaimed your axe and procured new armor for you as well. Better than that, I have twenty of my best men waiting for your command."

Chapter 10

As the two walked back up the winding stairs to the ground floor of the courthouse, guards stepped aside, bowing reverently at the sight of their king. They left the courthouse and stepped out into the cool, evening air. The king pointed to a building across the wide dirt road.

"My men are there," he said.

People all around stopped and stared at the two of them as they crossed the street. Aikur could see them whispering, but he didn't care what they were saying. His only thoughts centered on the hopes of rescuing his family. The king led Aikur into the building through a large door and then closed it afterward. Aikur and the king were met by a group of twenty men, each clad in armor and wearing swords, bows, and axes. On a long wooden table in the center of the room, Aikur spied his belongings. He moved swiftly, purposefully to the table where he found his armor and weapons waiting for him just as the king had said. He pulled on the thick leather hauberk and tightened the straps at his left side for a secure fit. Next he slid the boots, with their studded leather shin guards, onto his feet. He then took up his battle axe, but then paused when the king bent down to a box at the end of the table and pulled out Aikur's cloak made from the fur of a Kottri.

"I was able to reclaim this," the king said.

Seeing the cloak reminded Aikur of Karyna, who had urged him to wear the cloak and take his place as part of the community. Perhaps, had he listened to her advice, she would still be alive. Yet, as he turned and allowed the king to place it upon him, he felt as though Karyna was near him even now, encouraging him for his final battle. "You have given me hope," Aikur told the king after the cloak's clasp was fastened.

"And take these other gifts, with my blessing," the king said.

Aikur looked to the other items on the table and nodded. He slipped his left arm into the straps on the back of a large, round shield and then examined the proffered helmet briefly before donning it, careful to clasp the strap under his chin. The last thing he took was a khilij, a slightly curved long sword with a pointed wedge near the top of the blade's back.

He held the blade up in the light, admiring the black, Telarian steel. Then he slid it into its scabbard and secured it around his waist so that the sword hung at his side.

"And the gauntlets," the king said with a smile.

Aikur pulled on the gauntlets, admiring their sturdiness and the gold etching design along the top that almost looked like feathers.

"You have given me enough already, I cannot ask your men to travel with me where I must go."

The king shook his head. "It is *I* who command them to go with you. The way to the door is treacherous. They will aid you in arriving there safely. They will then wait for you for three days. Once you have your family, they will escort you to Belknap to meet with my priests."

Aikur pulled the parchment out and read the first few lines once more. "The back door to Hammenfein is lost in the fire pits of Deuldoran, in the southern most mountains that touch the seas upon the island of Mat'Jhar." He then skipped down to the bottom of the parchment. "Items needed are a cloak woven from the white hair of the fair elves, the scale of a leviathan, and the twisted horn of a great albino ram that roams the elven forest." Aikur looked

124

up to the twenty men around him. Then he read the rest of the parchment. "The cloak shall make the wearer invisible to mortal eyes as well as the eyes of the Bloodguards that patrol Hammenfein. The leviathan scales will enable the wearer to see hidden ghosts. The horn shall be fastened to a pole and fashioned into a spear. This spear will have the power to slay spirits, and send them to the void where they shall live no more, and vanish into nothingness." Aikur folded the parchment and put it back into his pocket. He gave a solid nod, then turned and bowed one more time to the king before marching out the door.

*****

The group travelled eastward, over the main road to Gilbrait. Soldiers in carts and on foot passed by them, heading back toward Lockleer for reprieve and healing. Several moans and wails came out from the backs of covered wagons.

"The battles have become fierce," one of the king's men said. "Since your attack on the goblin mines east of Oakhaven, the lines along the front have broken, and the armies have had to fall back."

"What happened?" Aikur asked. When he had been captured by Captain Marsten, there was no danger to anyone in the forests.

"Apparently a pair of female goblins managed to escape and find others to come to their aid. A group of orcs, accompanied by a trio of ogres, has amassed along the front and conducted several successful counter attacks. It looks like the border will hold, but Oakhaven has been evacuated."

Aikur nodded, but he said nothing. He didn't detect any anger in the man's voice, yet he couldn't be sure that he wasn't blaming him for the recent course of events.

Fortunately, the warrior ended the curiosity with his next words.

"The king has sent for reinforcements," he said staunchly. "We have bolstered the defenses and purchased enough time for the wounded to be carried back here where they might receive aid that otherwise they would not. The king has also called for Captain Marsten's arrest, and is in the process of pulling back from the front lines while negotiating a peaceful resolution. Last I heard there were some elves who can speak goblin tongue sent out to resolve the misunderstanding. The war will end soon enough, though it is an ugly business."

Aikur nodded. "That I can agree with," he said. "War is very ugly. That is why I wanted no part of it."

The two fell silent then and they continued marching along the road until it was night. As the moon and stars hung in the sky above, they made a fire and pitched camp. It was then that Aikur noticed each of the king's men had a small sack slung across their backs. From the sacks they pulled food; bread and dried meat mostly, but some had apples or other fruit to augment their meals. Aikur felt a coarse rumbling in his stomach, but he was not about to ask for someone to share with him. That was not his way. He started to look around, thinking about where he might find some food, when someone tapped on his shoulder.

Aikur turned to see a young man in his early twenties holding a sack out for him. "The king instructed me to carry this for you, it has the provisions for your journey."

Aikur looked at him quizzically. "Where is your food?" he asked.

The young man offered a half smile and turned to reveal a second pack still hanging on his back. "I have my own as well."

The Konnon warrior took the bag with a thankful nod. "My thanks for this," he said. "From now, I will carry it myself, no need to carry anything for me."

The young warrior nodded. "As you wish," he said. Then he pulled his own bag and started to rummage through for some food.

The two sat together in the cool grass, eating bread and dried beef. Aikur found three bottles of water in his sack, so he pulled one out and drank from it. He watched the young man eat silently, wondering where he was from, and why he had chosen this particular profession.

The young soldier looked up and smiled. "I am a bit young compared to the rest, I know," he said quickly. "Most of the other veterans in this group are more than ten years my senior, and they have many scars to show for it as well."

"Yet you sit among them; surely that must speak to your skill and prowess on the battlefield, does it not?" Aikur asked.

The young man shrugged. "I am stronger than some I suppose," he said.

"Young, *and* humble, that is not an oft found combination, especially among warriors," Aikur noted. The young warrior chuckled to himself and took another bite of bread. "What is your name?" Aikur asked.

"I am Finnigrel," the young warrior said.

Aikur paused, waiting for more. When Finnigrel continued eating instead of introducing himself further, he nudged the young man on the arm for more information. "Where were you born? Who is your father?"

Finnigrel shrugged. "You'll have to forgive me, it isn't that I mean to be rude, it's just that I don't rightly know. So, while another might say he is Finnigrel, the son of some great lord from some honorable, beautiful land, I am just Finnigrel. I was left on a doorstep when I was a few months old. I was raised in several different monasteries, and then I became a soldier."

"If raised in a monastery, why not become a monk?" Aikur asked.

Finnigrel shrugged. "Seems to me that a sharp sword or a strong fist usually stops the wolves of the world faster than throwing old tales and books." Finnigrel swallowed an enormously large, half-chewed mouthful of dried meat and then washed it down with a quick swig from his water jug. "I was never much for sitting still anyway. This way I can see the world, and I help people when I can. I may not preach and save souls, but I fight to protect lives. That has to be worth something, am I right?"

Aikur thought for a moment and then nodded. "It is a better reason than most for picking up the sword," he admitted.

"I bet you have some tales to tell," Finnigrel said excitedly. "When did you leave New Konnland?"

Aikur looked off to the fire and his smile faded to a stoic, solemn expression. "It was several years ago. My wife and I had no children yet, but we knew we wanted to have some. We also knew that our way of life was not what we wanted to give them. We wanted something better for them than what we had. So, when a shipment of supplies came in from the mainland, we bought passage back." He set his food down and sighed. "Our families disowned us, said we were abandoning them and our heritage. We didn't care. After arriving in Stoktown, I took my savings and bought a wagon and supplies. We traveled east for many months along the roads until we arrived in Gilbrait. Once there, we went to the governor's steward, who in turn directed us to Wallace, the town master of Oakhaven. We spent a week traveling and then purchased the deed to a healthy plot of land in the mountains, near where the front lines are now. We built a home, and planted gardens and trees. It wasn't long before we were pregnant. Life was good. We had peace, we had a family, and we had our own piece of heaven right here, nestled in the mountains of Kelsendale." His voice cracked and his eyes welled with tears. He couldn't continue speaking.

Finnigrel leaned over and laid a hand on Aikur's shoulder. "What happened to you wasn't right, not in the slightest," he said. "Every man here volunteered to come with you and help set it right, myself included. Furthermore, the king had no knowledge of what that coward Consuert did to make you fight the goblins. We'll get them back, no matter what it takes."

Aikur nodded, but he couldn't bring himself to look up at the young man. He choked back the tears, not willing to let them fall. Finnigrel stood and left Aikur alone.

After he walked away, Aikur pulled the transcription out to study it. He looked over the items he needed, and where to find them. Another warrior approached him from the left and pointed to the transcription.

"Do you think it is possible?" the warrior asked.

Aikur shrugged. "I am not for knowing," he replied honestly. "I have never dealt with elves, nor have I ever tried to walk among the fire pits of Mat'Jhar." Aikur folded it over once and swallowed while he thought. "I suppose I would try anything at this point."

The young warrior nodded and knelt down next to him. "May I see it?" he asked.

Aikur eyed him warily.

The young warrior nodded. "I will be careful with it," he promised. "I just like to know what I am getting into." Aikur held out the transcription and the young warrior slowly mouthed through the words as he read it to himself. He stopped abruptly and showed a line to Aikur. "How are we supposed to get the leviathan scales?" The warrior shook his head incredulously and ran a hand through his hair. "It says to play a series of notes using a flute made of the tusk of a narwhal. There are no such beasts in our oceans."

Aikur nodded knowingly and took the transcription back. "I know where we can acquire such a flute."

"Where?" the warrior asked.

Aikur smiled. "I have heard tales of an ifrit who carries exactly such a flute. My people knows of ifrits because we had to battle many of them when we first settled New Konnland. They were tricksters and thieves, reveling in the chance to murder innocent people for pleasure. But don't worry, we don't have to go to New Konnland to find one. The merchant ship we bought passage on to Kelsendale had a pair of bards. They sang often of the ifrit, and spoke of several people who had fallen victim to him. He roams the deserts near the well of Akoranth."

"An ifrit?" one of the warriors asked.

"How can you trust in a bard's song?" another asked.

"Don't worry, my people have a lot of knowledge about the ifrit. Everything the bards said in their tales matched the description of the ifrits we speak of back on New Konnland. I have a plan to defeat him and get both the flute, and the scales."

The young warrior shrugged. "Well, I am not one for tucking tail and running. If there is a back door to Hammenfein, I want to be named as one of the warriors brave enough to find it." With that, he rose to his feet and left Aikur to his thoughts. Aikur watched him go and then surveyed the camp. The others were all preparing to bed down for the night. He decided to do the same. He lay on his back and watched the stars until his eyelids finally closed and the thoughts raging in his mind quieted enough for him to slip into the land of dreams.

Chapter 11

The men rose with the sun the next morning and marched with new vigor, quick to pass the southern edge of Cherry Lake and through the dense forest as they kept up a grueling pace for the mountains of Kelsendale.

They arrived in the foothills shortly before dusk. The smell of fire and death hung heavily on the foggy air. Ruined pickets and overturned wagons dotted the landscape, along with newly dug mounds of dirt heaped up with a helmet or a sword marking each. Carrion birds circled overhead and a pair of wolves prowled the ground below.

"The orcs must have given Captain Marsten's men a harder fight than the man had prepared for," Finnigrel said.

Aikur nodded soberly. "All of this could have been avoided if only Consuert had contained his greed." Aikur reached back to touch the shaft of his axe. "Be vigilant. We may very well need to defend ourselves as we cross the mountains."

Aikur led the men quietly beyond the battle field and into the trees at the base of the mountains. No fires were lit that night, for fear it may draw attention to them. Aikur stood first watch, sitting up in a birch tree and looking down at the forest floor. The night was calm and cool, and silent. The moon danced in and out of the long silvery clouds above as the night dragged on.

The next morning the men were up and trekking through the woods. They followed a small stream up over a hillside of dead leaves and twigs. The walked for hours before they neared the top of the first mountain, it being roughly a third as tall as the mountains behind it, with the sun well overhead. Just as they were about to crest over the peak, Aikur signaled for the men to stop. He couldn't be certain, but he thought he had seen a large shadow move along the peak. Aikur signaled again and two of the king's men broke off to the left to flank around and scout. Another went to the right. Aikur slowly slid his black sword out from its scabbard and held it at the ready.

The men disappeared over the top, keeping low with the brush.

Aikur strained his ears, listening for anything that could clue him in to what lay ahead. The hairs on the back of his neck rose to stand on end. His instincts told him something was wrong. He started up the hill, running silently with his blade ready.

"Giant!" a shout called out from over the top of the slope. The scream was followed by one of the king's men flying out over the slope, crashing through branches and landing grotesquely several yards beyond the group. Aikur could hear the other warriors grunting and dodging while a heavy, lumbering thump crashed through trees and stone.

No sooner had he reached the top than he saw a fat, enormously thick, giant. It stood half as tall as the nearby pines and birch trees, and its arms were easily as thick as the biggest tree trunk. He wielded a crude hammer made from a log with a large stone secured to the top. He swung wildly at the other two that had gone ahead to scout, narrowly missing them as they flipped and somersaulted this way and that.

"Arrows!" Aikur commanded. Not more than two seconds later a slew of arrows flew through the air. The giant managed to knock some of them away with his massive hammer, but a few hit their mark and dug in deeply through his gray-blue flesh. The giant roared and tore the shafts from his side. Then he charged.

"Aim for his head!" Aikur shouted. None of them had enough time to fire. The giant was upon them in three steps, swinging his massive hammer down and forcing the men to scatter for their lives. Aikur was used to dealing with such foes, however. So when he dodged, he lunged in closer. He slashed out at the inside of the giant's left shin, then he spun around and hacked into the giant's right hamstring. His sword bit deep into the flesh and spilt a generous amount of the brownish-red blood, but the giant did not stop. He kicked and fought, forcing Aikur to jump away.

An axe flew through the air and landed solidly in the back of the giant's left shoulder. The monstrosity wheeled around screaming and howling, spit and slobber flinging out from his inflamed gums and lips. Another warrior ran in close, leaping up to bury his spear into the giant's protruding belly. The giant reflexively swatted the man away, sending him crashing into a nearby tree.

"The eyes!" Aikur shouted as he signaled for more arrows.

The giant was slowing now, and could not stop more than a couple of the arrows that assailed him from every direction. The steel heads tore into the flesh around his neck and head. The beast screamed horribly and tumbled backward down the slope, crashing to a stop against a large birch tree.

Aikur, unsatisfied with leaving the giant alive, sprinted down the hill, jumped atop the great foe and plunged his sword straight down into its heart. The giant's gray eyes went wide for a moment, and then it exhaled its final, foul breath and went limp.

The king's men gathered around and then moved to fetch the wounded. To their dismay, the other two were dead. The first that had been thrown had his neck and back broken in several places. The second had likely died when hitting the tree, as his head was smashed in and his skull was no longer intact.

"They died bravely," Aikur said. "A giant is no easy foe to slay, much like a minotaur in New Konnland." He looked around to the others and nodded admiringly. "I would not think less of any man here if he wished to return home. This fight is not yours, and I cannot ask you to continue on with me."

Finnigrel stepped in and spoke up first. "You didn't ask us to do it, the king asked for volunteers. We are with you until the end." The others nodded and grunted their agreement.

Aikur wiped his sword on the giant's leather breeches and then slid it back into his scabbard. "You are honorable warriors that any Konnon commander would be happy to take into the fold in New Konnland," he said. They spent the next several hours burying the dead and giving them their final rites. Then, they travelled on to To'ander, a city of the elves nestled in the great oak forest in the mountains.

No sooner had they entered the wood when a she elf appeared from behind an enormous oak tree. She wore a gown of silk, sky blue and shimmering in the sunlight. A great crown of emerald green sat upon her head and a long scimitar hung from her left hip.

"I am Tilwylen," she said softly. "I have received word from the king of the humans that you would be coming here."

Aikur stepped forward and the others stood still, watching the trees. "I have come to ask a favor," Aikur said. "I need a cloak."

Tilwylen held up her slender hand and pressed her fingers to Aikur's lips. "You desire a cloak woven from an elf's white hair." She let her hand slide down and gently brush Aikur's chest before she stepped around his side, surveying the warrior carefully. "And what will you do with such a prize?"

"The cloak will help me sneak by the sentinels in Hammenfein," Aikur replied openly. "If the king told you I was coming, then surely he told you of my plight."

The elf nodded and bit her lower lip as she completed a circle around the warrior. "What you ask is not so easily done as shearing a sheep," she said. "An elf's hair is inherently imbued with magic, and as such it augments the abilities of the elf. The longer the hair, and the brighter the color, the more benefit the elf may draw upon. To ask for enough white hair to make an entire cloak is to ask much."

Aikur nodded and knelt reverently. "I know it is not a simple trinket for which I ask, but I must have it. My wife and child even now are held in Hammenfein without cause, other than the fact that no one performed their final rites for them upon their deaths. Are there any among your people who would take pity on them, and weave for me this cloak, so I may free them from bondage? I will bring the cloak back to you after my family is safe."

Tilwylen nodded and stepped in close to Aikur, raising him up with her delicate, yet strong hands. "I have a proposition for you," she said. "If you can perform a task for me, then I will have the cloak made for you."

"Anything, and I will do it."

"Come lie with me, in the meadow yonder," Tilwylen said. "Our city has not seen the likes of your kind for many century, and it would please me well."

Aikur pulled away from her and furrowed his brow. "I cannot do this," he said.

Tilwylen cocked her head to the side and pursed her lower lip. "Am I not beautiful?" she asked.

Aikur nodded. "You are indeed, but I am not free to give myself. I am married."

The elf folded her arms and narrowed her olive shaped eyes at the warrior. "Your wife is dead," she said flatly. "There is no wrong in it."

Aikur shook his head. "Her spirit yet lives, and even should I fail in rescuing her, I could not dishonor our love like this." He took a step back, still shaking his head. "I am sorry, but if this is your price, then I will take my chances without the cloak."

"Then you will be caught, and tormented for an eternity in the halls of Hammenfein along with your family," Tilwylen said.

"But my honor shall be intact," Aikur replied. "I will find a way." He turned to walk away, but Tilwylen appeared directly in front of him in the blink of an eye.

"Fear not, honorable warrior, for it was only a test." She gestured to the forest beyond and the trees slid aside to open a path. "Come, let us all go to my city, and we shall weave this cloak for you."

"A test?" Aikur repeated.

The she elf nodded. "A gift so mighty, should only be bestowed upon one who knows the true value and meaning of virtue," she replied. "Come, tonight you shall eat and rest while we prepare the garment."

The band of warriors followed the she elf through the magical path in the wood until they came to a city of green stone buildings. The beautiful elves danced about them in reception and set a grand feast upon a long table made from a great fallen tree. The scent of roast pig, venison, and pheasant teased Aikur's nostrils while fruits and breads were laid out in abundance before them. The band drank deeply of sweet berry wine and ate their fill until all fell asleep in the cool grass under the white stars.

It was then, after the band of warriors had drunk themselves to sleep, that Tilwylen invited Aikur to accompany her to a small pool of water where three other elves were gathered. The four elves each took a pair of shears and cut the hair from their heads as Aikur watched. They sang a sad song that filled the air with grief at the loss of their hair, yet as they finished and took the pile down to a grand loom made of gold and brass, they did change their songs to a happy melody of family and glory. Thus did they sing as they toiled all the night long to fashion a cloak for Aikur while the large Konnon warrior fell asleep.

As the sun rose, Tilwylen laid the cloak over Aikur and bent down to kiss his forehead. "May the gods be with you on your quest," she said. Then she, and all of her city, disappeared into the forest once more, and the band of warriors woke to find themselves alone, lying near trees and under bushes in the wood.

Chapter 12

"What manner of magic is this?" one of the warriors said as they woke from their sleep.

"It matters not," Aikur said. "We have what we came for." He rose and fastened the cloak across his shoulders. The shining fabric was cool to the touch, and almost weightless. As he closed it around himself, the other warriors marveled and pointed with their fingers.

"He's gone!" one of them said.

Aikur opened the cloak and the others smiled widely. "So it works then?" Aikur asked. The warriors nodded. Aikur then removed it from his shoulders and rolled it up to place it into his pack. "Onward, we must move to the edge of the sea."

The group travelled to the south, and then eastward. They came to Duerbet and restocked with supplies. Then they continued on to the deep, jagged canyons near Blanche Peak. They skirted along its southernmost edge, between the end of the canyons and the cliffs overlooking the sea. Here they began to search the dry sands, looking for any sign of desert dwellers, for they sought a particular well. They searched for days under the hot sun, taking refuge in whatever shade they could find. On the third day, their water skins ran dry and their bodies soon tired of thirst. Aikur searched the desert, looking for any sign of plant life or animals, but he could find nothing. They pushed eastward as long as their feet would carry them, and then fell down upon the sands, exhausted and dying for thirst.

"Perhaps this won't work," one of the men said. "Maybe it is better that we go and challenge the leviathan ourselves, rather than perish in the desert."

Aikur shook his head. "The leviathan would make mincemeat of us without much effort," he said. "But if we find the well, we will have an advantage."

"What advantage?" Finnigrel asked.

"Just trust me," Aikur said with a wink. "I will search the dunes. I should be able to find the well. The rest of you wait here for a while." Aikur hiked and trekked around the dunes for another hour before he too finally became exhausted. He sat in the dirt at the base of a large dune and sighed.

At that moment, a black beetle burrowed up out from the ground and bit Aikur's left hand. He shook the insect away and cursed it, wishing it to leave him alone. The beetle laughed and jumped at him again, biting his stomach. Aikur jumped up, swatting at the beetle. The black bug opened its wings and started to fly around him, occasionally darting in and biting Aikur's face and neck. Aikur, enraged by the insect's behavior, chased it with his sword, swinging and slashing at it. The bug darted this way and that, leading him farther away from the group and up over a nearby dune. As soon as Aikur crested over the dune, the beetle dove down into the sand and burrowed out of the warrior's reach.

"Cursed pest!" Aikur shouted. He slid his sword back into its scabbard and then shook his head, looking around at the land before him. A smile stretched his dry and cracked lips when he saw a stone well sitting at the base of the dune surrounded by a patch of green grass and a large shrub. Aikur turned around and shouted for the men to catch up with him. They came running up over the dune and they all made their way to fill their water skins at the well.

As they stood drinking from the well of Akoranth, an ifrit appeared over them, laughing and sneering down at them. The ifrit had the face of a man, topped with the horns of a goat. The body was like a man's, but much larger and the skin was red, and the beast's legs ended in a pair of cloven hooves that sparked when it walked upon the ground.

"Who dares to steal my water?" the ifrit demanded. "I am the master of this desert, and you are trespassers here!"

The warriors moved their hands to their weapons, ready to fight, but Aikur held out a hand to stay the men.

"I know of his kind," Aikur said. "Let me speak with him."

The ifrit produced a large staff in one hand, and a flaming sword in the other. "What price do you offer me for my life-sustaining water which you have stolen?" the demon asked.

Aikur spied the ifrit's flute of bone upon its hip, and he smiled. "I have a gift to offer you," Aikur said. "Oh mighty spirit, we did not come to steal, but we knew of your generosity and kindness, for your fame has been spread far and wide across the desert."

The ifrit smiled at the praise, but did not altogether drop its guard. "What gift did you bring me?"

Aikur stretched out his arms. "I have a song for you."

"A song?" the ifrit mocked. "I can play my own songs. I prefer blood. Offer me four of your men, and I will let the rest of you leave in peace."

Aikur shook his head. "My song is great, the likes of which you have never heard," he said.

The ifrit shook its head. "No, I am the best flute player in all of the sands."

Aikur pointed to the flute. "Then, I have a wager for you," he said, for he knew how much ifrits loved bets. "Come and play your flute, and then I shall play. If my song is better than yours, then we all go free."

"And if mine is better than yours?" the ifrit asked with an arched brow.

"Then you may have all of our heads," Aikur assured him.

The ifrit nodded enthusiastically and stuck out his hand. "Then it is decided. Let us play here and now."

Aikur shook his head. "No, let us go to the cliffs that overlook the sea. I promise my song will be so marvelous that it will cause the sea itself to dance for you." Aikur could see the greedy desire in the ifrit's eyes. The demon agreed to follow them all to the cliffs and then played his song for them. The flute sent out the most beautiful notes over the sea. Many of the warriors wrung their hands with worry, not believing that Aikur could play better.

When the song finished, the ifrit smiled and handed the flute to Aikur. Aikur pulled the parchment from his pocket and played tune written thereon. The ifrit laughed at the melody's simplicity and licked its lips with desire. The large ifrit moved in, eager to collect its reward. Suddenly the seas stirred and a great blue beast raised its head over the cliffs.

The ifrit looked upon the leviathan and smoke billowed out from the demon's nostrils. The ifrit cracked its whip, but the leviathan opened its fang-filled jaws and spewed water at the demon. Aikur and the others backed away from the beasts while the two of them battled mightily. The ifrit dodged two lightning fast strikes from the leviathan, and the large serpent took a punishing blow to the side from the ifrit's fiery sword. A pair of scales fell from the leviathan and landed on the sand nearby.

As the two monsters battled, Aikur nimbly dashed in and took the scales, somersaulting across the sand and dust as he narrowly avoided the ifrit's flaming whip. He gently slid the scales into his backpack and then moved back to where the warriors stood watching the two great beasts fight.

141

Aikur took a spear from one of the warriors with him and launched it at the ifrit's leg. The spear pierced through the demon's right hamstring and caused the mighty beast to stumble, thus affording the leviathan a perfect opening. The great sea snake struck down in one mighty blow and seized the ifrit in its mouth. It ripped the demon from the ground and pulled him into the sea below, coiling and squeezing the fiery demon as it disappeared into the depths.

"It worked," Finnigrel said. "That was amazing."

Aikur nodded his head. "The note says that the song is a call for the leviathan, one that Kyra used to play with her flute." The mighty warrior shook the dust from his trousers and the group pressed on to the east.

"We must go into Tanglewood Forest," Aikur said. "There we shall find the third and final item for the quest. Afterword we will go to Tirnog, and purchase a ship from the elves there so we can sail to Mat'Jhar."

The group marched out from the desert and into the enchanted, elven forest. They knew better than to hunt game in the forest of the elves, for the elves that lived here forbade such activities to those not of elfish blood. However, they were able to pick berries and fruits from trees and bushes, which they knew were freely offered to all who passed through the forest.

After two nights and a day, they came to the city of Taron. Its alabaster spires reached high up through the giant redwoods and pointed into the heavens. None of the buildings had any visible corners. All of them were made to mimic the conical shells found upon beaches. Some had carvings in their sides, with jewels placed therein, while many of the buildings were simple and smooth, shining like crystals in the middle of a brown and green sea of trees.

Aikur spied many Vishi'Tai walking calmly between the many spires and towers. He saw no weapons upon any of the people he watched, which was something he found both strange and admirable.

"Imagine a city where no one carries their sword in the open," Aikur commented softly.

"But do they do it because it is safe, or because weapons are forbidden them?" Finnigrel asked.

Aikur turned and shook his head. "No, the elves of Taron are not disarmed by rules or overbearing rulers. They simply have no need to carry them."

"Aye, but I would wager their magical abilities would make up for any lack of steel," Finnigrel put in.

The Konnon warrior offered a short nod. "Likely so," he agreed. "Let us lay our weapons here by this tree, and then we will approach the city. The other warriors were reluctant at first, but when they all saw how quickly Aikur relinquished his own arms, the others followed suit. Unarmed, they walked into Taron openly.

The Vishi'Tai paid them no mind at first. The elves walked by the intruding group of humans without hardly glancing in their direction. It was quite unnerving, actually, to be ignored as though some insignificant insect. They stood in the center of the city, near a grand fountain which displayed a mermaid spouting pure, crystal-clear water from her mouth. The elves continued to walk by, despite a few attempts to stop one or two of them.

Finally, Aikur's patience was depleted. He stood atop the rim of the fountain and shouted out at all passersby. "Is there no hospitality to be found among the high elves of Taron? Are they so preoccupied with themselves that they have become devoid of compassion for others?"

His words stopped all around them and the elves each turned to face him with open disgust clearly displayed on their sharp, angular features.

"I have come in respect, leaving our arms and shields without the city as is your custom. Yet, I have not received even a tenth of the welcome I would receive should I enter a pig's wallow in the poorest of human villages in Kelsendale, though I be covered with muck and blood from battle. How has the great, majestic city fallen into such apathy?"

More elves gathered around, some whispering among themselves, but none answering Aikur's accusations.

"Were we not brothers in the War of Ire?" Aikur asked. "Did we not advance in the marred lands together during the Battle of Princes?" Aikur held his arms out wide. "Yet here I am no brother. I am ignored as a stray, and viewed with disdain as if I have fouled your city somehow with my presence. What is this evil you offer me?"

One of the elves, an exceptionally tall, golden haired man with slender cheeks and pointed jaw came out from the crowd to address Aikur. "What have we to do with thee?" The elf turned to regard the warriors. "I fought in the Battle of Princes, and my father and grandfather fought in the War of Ire. You were not there, though true it is that your ancestors were. You have no claim to such grand hospitality as you boast. Where are your deeds, that we may find thee equal to the fair elves of Taron?"

Aikur jumped down from the fountain and approached the tall elf. The dark skinned warrior looked up to the elf's light blue eyes. "In my teens I fought against an invading army of Kottri upon the lands of New Konnland. In my twenties I slew three minotaurs with not but a spear and a dagger. In my thirties I sailed against the corsairs that ravaged our coasts, and the coasts of Kelsendale. Now I am here, with a letter from the High King of Kelsendale, and you ask me to prove myself to you?" Aikur pulled the note from his pocket and showed it to the elf. "I seek the golden horn of the albino ram that roams these woods. I am here to ask for permission to hunt the animal."

The elf shook his head. "No. Jaeger forbids it. We refused to allow Kyra this hunt, why would we change our minds and allow a human to defile our forest?"

Finnigrel stepped forward and whispered into Aikur's ear. Aikur listened and nodded. "Very well, no hunting then," he said.

The elf arched his brow ever higher. "It is time for all of you to leave."

"What if we were to capture the ram and take one of its horns?"

"No," the elf said. "If you attack the ram, Jaeger will protect it."

"Jaeger?" Aikur asked. "Who is this, and may I speak with him?"

"Jaeger is the protector of Toran. He was there in the beginning with Lysander, and is here still. You may not speak with him, nor may you have the horn. Be gone, we cannot help you."

Aikur set his jaw and stared at the elf. He had half a mind to pummel the arrogance out of the fair elf's head, but opted instead to leave in order to conceive a new plan. He glanced to Finnigrel, thinking on the words the young warrior had whispered to him moments before. Aikur and the others walked back out of the town and retrieved their equipment. None of them spoke as they strapped their weapons back on and prepared to travel.

"What will we do without the spear?" one of them asked.

"Finnigrel had an idea about that," Aikur said with a nod.

The young warrior smiled and nodded. "In the monastery where I grew up, there was a book that discussed the albino ram. Apparently the animal is worshipped to some degree by the elves here. Every century, it sheds its horns, like a deer might."

145

"But rams don't shed their horns," one of the warriors put in.

"This one does," Finnigrel said.

"So we are going to search the forest for shed horns? How would we know where to look?"

Finnigrel shook his head. "No, the elves here always take the shed horns and put them in their shrine."

"So we are to steal it?" another warrior asked.

Finnigrel nodded.

Aikur led the group around the elven city. As they passed by the eastern most edge and the moon rose high above the city, Finnigrel peeled off from the group and snuck into the city. Aikur instructed the others to continue onward toward Tirnog and wait for him to catch up with them. Then he donned the cloak of invisibility and followed after Finnigrel to watch over the young warrior.

The young man crept along the shadows, being careful not to make a sound as he stole his way into the shrine through an open window. He padded softly along the stone floor, scanning the stone walls, the pedestals holding curious artifacts, and the paintings and murals on the ceiling and floor. There were no pews or chairs in the shrine. Only a star shaped pillow in the center, at the feet of a giant marble statue of a tall elf.

Finnigrel studied the statue and smiled when he saw what the statue was holding in its hands. There, in its open palms, lay the golden horn of the albino ram. Finnigrel grappled with the slick stone, trying to find purchase to climb the structure. Each time he jumped up, he slid back down to the floor. Luckily, he was able to steady each fall so that he barely made any more noise than a heavy footstep. After a few unsuccessful attempts, he grabbed a book from a nearby pedestal and took aim at the horn. The young warrior deftly threw the book so that it struck the statue, and in its rebound knocked the horn out over the floor. He caught the horn, but the book crashed to the floor, creating a dull echo in the shrine.

"Is someone in there?" a voice asked from without.

Finnigrel sprinted for the window and leapt out. As he hit the ground outside, he could hear the heavy brass door opening inside. He didn't wait to see if they noticed what he had done. He sprinted for all he was worth to reach his comrades.

A few seconds after he entered the forest, he heard a great bugle blast, and he knew that his theft had been discovered. Into the forest he dashed, zig-zagging through the trees and praying that he would be faster than his pursuers. Soon he could hear shouts and whistles behind him, and he knew he was still a long way off from the group.

Suddenly a nimble elf dropped from a tree above and drew his bow back, aiming a deadly arrow at Finnigrel's throat. "Stop or die, thief!"

Finnigrel stopped, sliding on the forest floor a couple of inches. "I need it," he pleaded. "We can return it, just let us borrow it."

"That horn provides our town with protection," the elf replied. "On your knees."

Suddenly, the elf's bow snapped in the middle and the arms of the bow flew back, one smashing into the elf's torso, and the other shattering his nose and dropping him back to the ground. An instant after the elf fell to the ground, his head suddenly jerked to the side roughly and then he exhaled.

"Stay still," Aikur commanded as he removed the cloak just enough to show his face to Finnigrel. Aikur then pulled the unconscious elf into the bushes and covered him as best he could.

"You kicked him?" Finnigrel said.

"I broke his bow too," Aikur replied.

"Where are the others?" Finnigrel asked.

Aikur rushed forward and used the cloak to cover them both. "They have moved on toward Tirnog. Remain quiet now."

A few moments later a pair of elves came near, scanning the area with bow and scimitar at the ready. Aikur used his hands to guide Finnigrel and the two of them silently escaped without detection. They used the cloak all the way to Tirnog, for fear of being discovered by the other elves, and were all too happy to see their comrades waiting for them with the King of Tirnog at the gates of the city.

Chapter 13

Aikur removed the cloak and walked openly to the elf king. "No need to hide here," Aikur said. "The elves of Tirnog are strong allies to the king."

Finnigrel nodded.

"The city of Tirnog welcomes its guests, and extends the warmest of wishes. May you have long life, and plentiful peace," the king greeted with open arms.

"May peace also find its way to your door, and never leave," Aikur replied with a nod of his head.

"It has been long since Tirnog has welcomed a Konnon within its walls," the king said. "Your men have told me of your quest, and I must say that I have no ship available to sell."

Aikur's countenance fell and his shoulders slumped. "Not even a boat?" he asked.

The king stepped forward and smiled as he put a hand on Aikur's shoulder. "Your men told me *everything* about your quest. I have no ship I would sell, for that would be robbing a man who has already lost so much. Instead, I offer my ship to you, free of charge. My personal guard will see you to the shores of Mat'Jhar, and they will wait for your return. Should you succeed, they will sail with you to Belknap as well, so your journey may be swift."

Aikur fell to his knees. "You have my gratitude, and anything you would ask of me is yours in return."

"Leave the horn with my men upon the ship when you disembark for Belknap," the king suggested. "Its

149

blessing will help protect us from evil spirits that lurk in the night."

"Agreed," Aikur promised.

The king snapped his fingers and another elf appeared, holding a splendid shaft. "Give him the horn, and he will fashion the spear you need." Aikur did so and the group went into Tirnog. They feasted, and prepared for the sea voyage, and then slept.

The next morning, they set out for Mat'Jhar. The elves masterfully navigated the winds and waves while Aikur and the warriors rested their legs and enjoyed the salty sea air. Some of the men played stretch, a knife throwing game where each contestant had to stretch to reach the opponent's knife with their foot once it was thrown without falling over. Most of the others sat upon crates or benches and simply watched the waves roll by.

Finnigrel soon found Aikur sitting at a small table, again reading the transcription. "Does it change each time you read it?" the young warrior asked.

Aikur smiled. "No, but I like to make sure I don't forget anything vital."

"Do you know what Mat'Jhar is like?"

The Konnon shook his head. "Only what I heard in tales and legends."

"They say the fire pits stretch across the southern half of the island, and that no plants can grow anywhere on the surface. It is rumored that fire demons roam there too, so I've heard."

"I suppose we shall soon find out for ourselves."

"Are you afraid to face the Bloodguard?" Finnigrel asked.

Aikur shook his head. "Without my family I am already dead," he replied. "There is nothing that the orcish spirit servants of Hatmul can do to me." Aikur patted the spear next to him and smiled. "Besides, I have the spear, thanks to you."

"You will earn much glory," Finnigrel said, ignoring the comment about the spear. "No one has ever willingly challenged the Bloodguard before. Only the most valiant orcish warriors can become members of the Bloodguard," Finnigrel said. "I can't imagine what you are going to see down there."

"Well, I will be relying on stealth more than this spear, truth be told. I don't want to sound any kind of alarm."

"I would go in with you," Finnigrel offered.

Aikur shook his head. "While I appreciate the gesture, I cannot allow it. This is for me to do alone."

Finnigrel's smile faded and he offered a simple nod before looking out to the waters. "There are dolphins out there," he noted. "I hear that is a good omen." Finnigrel then went back to join the others playing stretch, pushing one of the players over onto his face and starting a minor scuffle. Aikur laughed to himself and then turned his attention back to the transcription. He studied it several times a day for the rest of the sea voyage.

The elves augmented the weather with a bit of their own magic bringing the group of heroes to Mat'Jhar within a week's time. They rounded the southern edge of the island and set anchor down while Aikur went ashore. While upon the ship, two of the elves had fashioned a visor from the leviathan's scale and fastened it to a helmet. They took care to ensure a proper fit for Aikur to wear the helmet. He looked quite peculiar as he reached the beach of the fire pits. His helmet resembled a bubble more than a piece of armor. The ram's horn spear glowed magnificently in the sunlight, but its tip was curled, instead of straight, and the cloak flapped in the breeze half covering Aikur in invisibility and creating the illusion that his legs and back were missing.

151

However strange he appeared, the landscape of southern Mat'Jhar was equally as extraordinary. A thick, silvery mist floated just above the red dirt and stone, splitting apart as geysers or vents would spew steam or fire into the air. Jagged, black rocks stuck out from the ground like broken spears that a giant might have pushed up from underground. As Finnigrel had said, there were no plants of any kind. There wasn't much of anything, actually, just smoke, mist, steam, fire, rock, and dirt.

On into the red lands of mist he went, holding his spear at the ready and closing the cloak around him to hide within its protection. He spied a pair of ghosts upon the surface of the fire pits. Each held a wickedly curved sword and appeared to be the spirit of an orc, for they had orcish forms, and they spoke in a strange tongue that he could not recognize.

Aikur crept up to them, not sure how well the cloak would work against ghosts, but when the spirits started floating his way without any sign of seeing him, Aikur walked upright and approached them quickly. It was time to test the spear.

He thrust out into one, expecting to feel nothing at all, but instead feeling resistance similar to striking a real body. However, instead of blood, light leaked from the ghost, and then the form faded. The second ghost wheeled around with its sword, but couldn't see Aikur to defend himself. Aikur swung his spear back to catch the second ghost across the neck, and it too vanished as had the first.

A smile crossed Aikur's face as he realized the plan had more merit than he had heretofore dared hope. He jogged to find the fire pit spoken of in the parchment. He studied the rock formations, looking for anything that might resemble a snake, as the parchment had noted that the rear entrance to Hammenfein lay deep within the smoking pit below the rock shaped like a viper. Once he finally discovered it, he jumped down into the smoldering chute, sliding down into the bowels of Terramyr.

The heat became exponentially more intense. Beads of sweat quickly turned into rivulets that streaked down across Aikur's face and dripped from his chin. At the bottom of the chute, fire spurted out from holes in the wall. One almost caught Aikur in the face, but he managed to duck under the burst without harm.

A trio of Bloodguards crossed the opening of the tunnel in front of him, talking amongst themselves and laughing as they took turns yanking on chains that were dragging a couple of condemned souls. Aikur thought to attack them and release the damned souls, but then changed his mind, preferring to keep his presence as unnoticeable as possible.

After the group passed out of sight down a side tunnel he crept along the cave to his left, careful to flatten himself against the wall whenever a Bloodguard or ghost came near. He walked for hours in the labyrinth, memorizing each turn as he went deeper into the hellish realm. Finally, he came out of the tunnels and saw a magnificent city before him. Black granite mixed with pink tufa forming a beautiful, yet horrific fortress before him. It looked as though the binding cement was made from red pumice, which shined like blood holding the stones together. The walls rose up about forty feet to just touch the roof of the chamber. A host of Bloodguards patrolled along the battlements, shouting and yelling things that the Konnon warrior could not understand.

Aikur moved in close to the giant, obsidian gates. Arcane symbols and runes that he did not recognize were carved in the archway over the gate, and glowed red like molten lava. He could hear shouting and wailing. Occasionally he heard the sound of cracking whips and horrid screams. He tried to put the sounds out of his mind and moved in to stand off to the side of the gates, waiting for the portals to open.

The pink and black walls seemed almost endless, going on for miles and disappearing in the depths of the red, fiery caverns before him. He wasn't even sure if his position in the tunnels was still under the island anymore, or if perhaps he had walked so far as to technically be under the ocean at the moment. Without the walls, there were Bloodguards everywhere. The horrible orcish soldiers wielded swords, pikes, axes, and every imaginable weapon. Some groups he could see were busy tormenting unfortunate souls with whips of fire. The Bloodguards made the spirits work, gathering stone and cutting more tunnels into the rock around them. Aikur didn't even dare to count the Bloodguards. There were legion upon legion on the outside of the walls alone. There was no way for him to know how many more might be inside. He pulled his cloak tighter around himself, thankful that he had not been discovered as of yet.

Finally, after what seemed like an hour or more of standing and dodging Bloodguards unaware of his presence, a large host emerged from one of the tunnels beyond the gate. One of the orcs blew a bugle, the low tone echoing clearly off the cavern walls. A loud gong sounded from within the walls and the gates opened. A flood of souls streamed out. The Bloodguards swooped down on them, cracking fiery whips and beating them with their hellish weapons. The souls all fell back like a wave, receding into the city of hell.

Aikur took his chance and slipped into the pressing throng. He ducked under weapons and carefully pushed through the condemned souls as he hurried through the open gates. A signal horn blasted a loud note and the crowds parted.

Scurrying up next to a wall, Aikur was careful to keep his breath quiet. A great figure in flowing, tattered robes floated above the ground, looking down upon the souls and the Bloodguards. He carried a large scythe, and his face was covered by a hood. Aikur knew at once it was Khefir, Hatmul's brother and the reaper of the damned.

The god bellowed a command in a language that Aikur could not comprehend. The Bloodguards all moved quickly and orderly, clearing most of the souls from the area, leaving only ten or so in the middle before Khefir. Aikur watched intently as Khefir conjured a tablet from thin air and approached the souls.

"Morgana Desirth," Khefir said in the Common Tongue as he approached one of the souls. "For the crimes you committed while in your mortal life, Hatmul has decreed that your punishment shall be eternity in Vishnar, the second level of hell."

The female spirit cried out in protest, but was quickly wrapped in fiery chains by a pair of Bloodguards and dragged off into a door on the far side of the courtyard.

Khefir moved to the next soul. "Maxim Kurian, for your crimes, you have been sentenced to an eternity in Hammenfein city, the first level of hell."

The male spirit hung his head, and accepted his fate as another pair of Bloodguards approached and wrapped him in fiery chains. They pulled him away into another door nearby where Aikur stood.

Khefir moved on through the next five souls, sending each to their predetermined fates. However, when the reaper stood before the last soul, he stopped and looked at the tablet for a few moments. It was then that Aikur noticed that the spirit of a Konnon man which stood before Khefir.

The reaper drew his hood back to reveal a bony skull, devoid of any flesh or tissue. The jaw clicked slightly as

Khefir spoke. "Ander Marzahn, you have lived an honorable life upon the mortal plane, but you are unfortunate to be cursed by your race. Those upon the mortal world failed to offer you final rites, and therefore your soul is forfeit to Hammenfein." Aikur could almost swear that Khefir would be frowning if he actually had a face to show emotion. The tone in the god's voice showed the slightest hints of empathy for the cursed Konnon.

"I accept my fate," Ander said proudly. He held his wrists out for the Bloodguards and nodded that he was ready to be taken to his place of torment.

"Take him to the chamber where such unfortunate souls are kept," Khefir said.

A single Bloodguard approached the Konnon spirit and took him by the arm, without chains, to a room farther down the east side. Aikur was quick to follow, hoping that perhaps his wife and children would be there as well.

The door opened and Ander walked in. Aikur slid by the Bloodguard just before the door closed and immediately jumped to the left to avoid bumping into a trio of Bloodguards who were waiting to receive Ander's spirit.

"Vidd ot alatti," one of the Bloodguards said as he pushed Ander's spirit forward with one hand and pointed with his other hand in a downward motion. The other two led the spirit down an iron staircase to a massive row of cells and rooms that seemed to go on endlessly. Aikur looked down and noticed that the Bloodguard who had given the command had a key attached to his belt. The Bloodguard turned then and looked right at Aikur.

Aikur's heart froze and his breath caught in his throat. The Bloodguard took a couple of steps toward him. Only when the Bloodguard looked down and fumbled with his keys did Aikur realize the guard could not see him, he was simply going to lock the door.

Aikur slipped out of the way and watched as the Bloodguard locked the door and then went to sit at a table nearby. The orcish brute filled a mug with something that looked like wine and took a long drink as he closed his eyes and relaxed his head on the back of the chair.

Aikur moved on to search the cells. He walked down the endless hall for hours, scanning each cell he passed, searching the myriad faces inside, but to no avail. He kept walking and searching until he found a side chamber. He went in and found a palatial room decorated with gold and gems in the walls. The furniture was exquisitely crafted, and the beds and couches appeared soft and luxurious with their many pillows and thick, inviting cushions. A few Bloodguards slept in the room. Some others lounged on the couches and ate fresh fruits from a platter of gold.

Aikur's stomach growled slightly at the sight of the food, but he pushed his hunger aside and moved on down the hall. He turned down a side corridor and saw many more holding cells. His heart sank within his chest and his hopes began to fade. It felt as though he would never find them. The halls of Hammenfein were much larger than he had ever anticipated.

At that moment, a group of three smaller souls crossed the corridor in front of him. One Bloodguard led the children. A chain of fire linked each of the souls by the wrists. Aikur could no longer hold his anger. He stalked the Bloodguard, waiting only until the group passed out of sight of the cells down a narrow corridor. The orc opened a cell and motioned for the children to walk inside. No sooner did the first child pass the orc than Aikur ran the golden ram's horn through the Bloodguard's chest. The orc's mouth twisted in agony, but no sound came out before the Bloodguard vanished. The children froze in place, staring at the empty air in front of them. Aikur unclasped his cloak just long enough to hold a finger over his mouth and quiet the children.

"I can help you," he told them, "but first I need some help from you." He told them of his wife and child. The young spirits told him they knew of a family that matched their description two corridors over. Aikur ushered the children into the cell and promised to be back once he had his family. He then fastened his cloak once more and started off.

He ran back to the junction with the other corridor and then continued on as the children had instructed him. When he arrived at the cell he found only three people inside. He saw his lovely wife sitting in the back, near the wall, talking in hushed whispers to Dezri, but there was another child with them. His heart skipped and his eyes welled with tears. Of course, Karyna had been pregnant. He was looking at the spirit of his unborn child, sitting there with his wife. A lump formed in his throat so that when he opened his mouth, he barely made more than a squeak.

Aikur scanned the hallway for guards and then cleared his throat. He whistled sharply and tapped his knuckles against the iron bars of the cell. His wife looked up and frowned. Realizing she couldn't see him, he unclasped his cloak and smiled as he gestured for them to be silent. His wife jumped up and ran to the cell door, tears upon her face.

"Tell me you are not dead," she cried. "Tell me you are still live!"

Aikur nodded and reached between the bars to take her hands in his, but he felt only cold as his physical hands passed through hers. "I am alive," he assured her. "I am here for you."

"No, you can't be here," she said. "They will catch you."

Aikur smiled. "The gods are on our side, my love."

"He te, mit kereshel betolakod?" an angry voice shouted from nearby.

Instinctively, Aikur jumped back from the cell and fastened the cloak, disappearing from the Bloodguard's view. The orc's hand went for a bugle at his hip, but Aikur was already upon him. He thrust his spear into the demon's neck before the warning could be sent. The spirit disappeared as all the others had, leaving only a golden key that fell upon the ground. Aikur took the key and ran to the cell door. He opened it and gathered his family under the cloak with him.

They had to walk slowly, otherwise the cloak would sway too much to cover their feet, but eventually they made it out of Hammenfein. Aikur escorted them all the way to the ship and all of the warriors shouted his praise. The elves hurried to cast off, but Aikur stopped them, telling them of his promise to the children that had helped him find his family.

Against the advice of the elves, and despite the protests from his own family, Aikur went back into the bowels of Hammenfein. He left Finnigrel in charge, and stipulated that they should cast off after he disembarked and keep a safe distance from Mat'Jhar, just in case he was discovered.

The elves did as he commanded, and took the ship out far enough that it was necessary to use a spyglass to scan the beach. They waited for the space of a day and a half. Finnigrel and the other warriors all prayed to the old gods for their blessings and Aikur's family maintained constant vigil from the bow.

Finally, Aikur appeared with the souls of forty children, and several Konnon adults who had done no wrong during their lives except for failing to have their final rites performed. He waved for the ship and the elves bolstered the sails with their magic, sailing in speedily as they could. They loaded the liberated souls and then set sail for Belknap with much haste.

The rest of the voyage was uneventful. The seafarers were met with fair weather and favorable winds. They made the journey to Belknap faster than expected, and the king's priests were there as promised.

After the ship was secured to the small, weather-worn dock, the other Konnon spirits ran down the planks and up toward the shrine. Aikur turned to the surviving warriors that had made the journey with him. He gave the spear to the captain of the ship as promised, so it could be given to the king at Tirnog. Then he removed his armor and laid it out upon a large wooden crate.

"See that these items get returned to the king," he said. The warriors each promised to see it done, and then Aikur turned to Finnigrel. "For you, take my axe, and take the flute," he said with a smile.

"Will you be all right now?" Finnigrel asked as he took the items in hand.

Aikur glanced to his wife and children and smiled. "We'll be just fine." He bade a final farewell and then walked with his family toward the shrine.

Karyna was quiet as the children played and ran about upon the grass, happy to once again be free. Aikur tried again to hold his wife's hand, but his physical form slid through her hand before he remembered that it wouldn't work.

"Soon," Karyna said.

Aikur smiled, and for the first time since that horrible morning, he felt peace in his heart.

They walked up to the shrine, which was much smaller than Aikur had expected. It was a building built of stone, about thirty feet high in the center, and built as if two square foundations had been laid out to arrange an eight-pointed star. The front door opened for the priests, and the other spirits were busy shouting and calling out as periodic flashes of light would burst from within the shrine and reach the doorway, casting blue and violet hues onto the grass.

As Aikur approached, he could see the priests giving each spirit their final rights. Each time they finished, a spirit would vanish from the shrine in a dazzling display of colorful lights. Both the young children and the adults praised Aikur as they made their final journey into Volganor.

Behind the priests stood a tall woman with white wings. She wore a steel helmet and breastplate, and carried a tall spear. She turned to meet Aikur's gaze and then walked toward him. The priest finished giving final rights to one of the spirits and another eruption of light tore through the darkness inside the shrine.

"I am Nagé," the tall woman said as she stopped inside the doorway, blocking Aikur's entrance.

"I am Aikur Anarin," Aikur said. "This is my family."

Nagé looked to Karyna and offered a nod. "You have done something that no other has ever been able to do," Nagé said. "You went into the bowels of Hammenfein and rescued others that had been trapped there."

Aikur nodded. "My wife and children are good people," Aikur said, hoping such an explanation would satisfy the goddess.

"All children are innocent, but the adults I must judge," Nagé said. She turned to Karyna and stared at her for a few moments. Then, a bright smile stretched the goddess' lips under the open-faced helmet. "You are indeed good. Go in, and you shall have your reward."

Karyna and the children walked into the shrine.

Aikur then took in a breath and looked to Nagé. "And may I go in as well?" he asked.

"You?" Nagé said. "You are not yet dead."

"Please, I have suffered enough. I wish to be with them."

Nagé reached out and placed a hand on Aikur's head. The large Konnon could feel a wave of warmth flow into him. "You have guilt," she said. "You have regrets and shame."

Aikur nodded. "There are things I have done that I am not proud of," he said.

Nagé continued. "Yet, you acted with honor. You were tricked into fighting the goblins, so there should be no shame for you in that. You also know that Icadion has decreed that all members of the cursed races should be destroyed, so fighting the goblins would not have kept you from Volganor in any case." She pulled her hand back and looked deeply into his eyes. "Moreover, even with everything you were put through, you did not let your vengeance control you in the end. You spared those who were not warriors, and you fought for peace before you were betrayed. You may hold your head high."

Nagé then extended the tip of her spear to touch Aikur's forehead. There was a dazzling, blinding flash of white light as Aikur's body fell to the ground behind him, and his spirit was left standing at the door of the shrine.

"Uzun do rath, mo keth dun soreen," Nagé said in the Konnon Old Tongue. "Azertu doraw, molith kun sinah."

Aikur felt a swell of energy embrace him.

"Come, you may enter Volganor," Nagé said. "Enter, and take your rest." Aikur stepped into the shrine and found his wife and children waiting for him. This time, when he took her hand, he was able to hold hers. He laughed and bent down to scoop up Dezri as Karyna held the younger baby in her other arm. Many colors rippled through the shrine as the rear wall fell away to reveal a bridge that appeared to be made of a rainbow.

"Let's go home," Karyna said. "We've missed you."

"And I have been lost without you." Aikur started to walk, but then Dezri punched him in the chest. Aikur turned on his son and saw the young toddler spirit giggling and smiling wide.

"I stwoooongeeeeerrrrrrrrr!"

Epilogue

Jaeger sat on a hilltop nearby, watching the smoldering fires die out over the city he had come to love. Toran was no more. He could still hear the angry shrieks and shouts of the demons that searched for the crystal even now.

"I'm sorry, Lysander, I failed." He looked down and plunged Myrskyn, Lysander's magical sword, into a stump. The gnome then turned to the albino ram and climbed atop the creature's back. With only one horn left in the city, the magic had failed to protect Toran, and the demons had come searching for the crystal Jaeger now held in his left hand. "Others may praise the name Aikur Anarin, but not I," Jaeger said. "I will curse the impulsiveness of humans, their lack of judgment, and their quickness to act without considering the repercussions of their actions."

Jaeger looked around, hoping to find some inspiration for where to go. It would be easier if Reshem appeared. Perhaps then Jaeger would be able to take some comfort in his actions. As it was, no one would be able to find him now. Not Lysander, nor Reshem. The gnome sighed and offered up a prayer to Mother Terramyr, then turned to cast one more longing glance toward the swaying columns of smoke rising up over the ruins of Toran.

"Come, ram, we need to find another place to hide," Jaeger said. The gnome patted the animal on the neck and it turned to flee. It sprinted over hill and vale, darting through the dense woods of the forest and outrunning even the swiftest of demons as they traveled southward toward the Murkle Quags.

About the Author

Sam Ferguson is the proud author of more than twenty fantasy novels. He launched his writing career with The Dragon's Champion series, cracking the Top 100 for epic fantasy books. He has also written The Netherworld Gate Trilogy, The Sorceress of Aspenwood Trilogy, and The Haymaker Adventures to name just a few. He has had several #1 best-sellers in the U.K. and Australia, as well as a couple of top 20 hits in the U.S.

Nearly all of his novels take place on Terramyr, a single world rife with varying races, religions, and conflicts that propel the world itself along through its timeline toward a final climax. So, while each novel or series can be savored on its own, the more a person reads, the more immersed they become with Terramyr, its gods, and the grand events that will ultimately prove the worth and decide the fate of its inhabitants. (Sam has also hidden a few Easter Eggs such as crossover characters and other fun tid-bits for the eager reader!)

In his free time, Sam Ferguson is a competitive powerlifter. While he spent his first career as a U.S. diplomat, living in Latvia, Hungary, and Armenia, he is now quite content to travel the far reaches of Terramyr instead, and hopes to bring many of you fun-loving adventure seekers along for the ride!

You can easily find Sam Ferguson's Facebook page, sign up for alerts on his Amazon page, or you can follow Sam on his author blog: www.talesfromterramyr.com

See the full collection of Dragon Scale Books by visiting: www.DragonScaleBooks.com:

About Terramyr

This book is a story from the world of Terramyr, a world which is part of a grand fantasy universe.* The world of Terramyr is rich in stories of adventure and magic, where struggles of the small and mighty alike are worthy of being told. Each story reflects a different point in time where the course of Terramyr's history is affected; all paths leading to a moment when the life of Terramyr will be weighed in the cosmic balance.

Terramyr is a palimpsest of fantastic history and magic, where different ages of gods and mortals have given rise to heroes and villains of all sorts, from each corner of the world.

The life of Terramyr is measured in five major eras of time, each a testament to the strength of will of mortals and those who would seek to become gods. Covering over 12,000 years of Terramyr's history the struggles of each race, from orcs to demigods, from elves to gnomes, are recorded by author Sam Ferguson.

We invite you to take a walk in the wild jungles of Prirodha, explore the verdant seacoast of the Elven Isles, climb the snowy peaks of the Dryden Range, delve the mighty caverns of the Dwarves of Roegudok Hall, discover the hidden treasures of the merpeople of the Ilion Ocean, and to share the adventures which take place in many more beautiful, exciting locations across the world of Terramyr.

You can learn more about the World of Terramyr at

Terramyr.wikia.com

And

www.WorldOfTerramyr.com

And

www.DragonScaleBooks.com

*Related worlds include Kendualdern, a world where dragons rule.

While each series or stand-alone book which is part of the World of Terramyr can be enjoyed on its own, the more you explore, the more you will find easter eggs, learn about the mythology and history of the world, and the more you may come to discover the extent of the powers interested in guiding Terramyr to its final end.

You can enjoy the stories in any order you choose, but for readers who are interested in knowing where in the chronology of Terramyr a given story falls, here is a chronological list of the stories (those currently available, and those yet to come) that take place on the World of Terramyr.

Pre–history and Creation Era	The Dragons of Kendualdern series Ascension Dominion: Seeds of Alliance

	Dominion 2: Edge of the Storm Dominion 3: Rise of an Empire (Summer 18) Hunted (Coming Soon) Rebellion (Coming Soon) Annihilation (Coming Soon) The World Seed (Coming Soon)
Ancient Era (1,000 years)	
Dark Ages aka The Era of Kings (3,500 years)	Flight of the Krilo (Year 365)
Age of Demigods (5,000 years)	The Haymaker Adventures (Year 3,500) The Sorceress of Aspenwood Series (Years 3,676 – 3,677) The Dragon's Champion Series (Years 3,709 – 3,711) Son of the Dragon (Year 3,710) The Ghosts of Kobhir (Year 3,710) The Wealth of Kings (Year 3,711) The Fur Trader (Year 3,720) The Fur Trader 2 (Year 3,720)
Common Era (1,700 years)	
Enlightened Era aka Age of Wonders (1,000 years...?)	

Other Books by Sam Ferguson:

The Dragon's Champion Series
The Sorceress of Aspenwood Series
Son of the Dragon
The Dragons of Kendualdern Series
The Fur Trader 1 & 2
The Haymaker Adventures
Hapless Heroes Series
Flight of the Krilo
The Ghosts of Kobhir
Gatekeepers
The Lost City of Alfarin
Wren and the Ravens
The Moon Dragon
The Beast of Blue Mountain

Other Books by Dragon Scale Publishing:

The Protector of Esparia by Lisa M. Wilson
Wisp the Wayfinder and Other Tales by J.M. Hauser
Kingdom of Denall Series by Eric Buffington:
Blood Bound by B. Griffin
Blood Penance by B. Griffin
Favored by B. Griffin
The Bohemian Magician by A.L. Sirois
Tharzule's Tome of Wishes by Malinda Smiley
Codex of Light by E.P. Stein
Codex of Darkness by E.P. Stein
The Dream Chest by E.P. Stein

For more, check out Dragon Scale Publishing's website:
www.DragonScaleBooks.com